DEATH ON 30 BEAT

DEATH ON 30 BEAT

MAYNARD COLLINS

DENEAU

1989

Deneau Publishers
760 Bathurst Street
Toronto, Canada
M5S 2R6

Copyright 1989

Covert Art: John Booth

Printed and bound in Canada

Canadian Cataloguing in Publication Data

Collins, Maynard
Death on thirty beat

ISBN 0-88879-186-0

I. Title.

PS8555.O55D43 1989   C813'.54   C89-093609-9
PR9199.3.C6D43 1989

Death on 30 Beat is a work of fiction in its entirety, in which fictional characters and historical personages exist side by side, acting and speaking solely at the whim of the author.

For Aaron and David,
and my sister, Christine

CHAPTER I

When you're dead, I guess it doesn't matter. But it's not a nice way to die, falling seven storeys onto the sidewalk.

Nineteen fifty-four was a long time ago. I hadn't thought about what happened that summer for over thirty years.

It was the television item that did it. I was reading the newspaper until I had to throw it down in disgust. That was my tax money the government was throwing away.

I flipped the television to channel four. They were doing one of those "This Day in History" items, and mentioned the diplomat who jumped from the seventh floor of the Chateau Laurier Hotel in Ottawa a long time ago.

I remember 1954 fondly. In those days, the finance minister used to get into trouble for bringing in too large a budget surplus. Not like these lamebrains today.

I got interested. They showed the Chateau Laurier, the Houses of Parliament, some stock footage of old cars and funny clothing, the prime minister giving one of his purposely boring speeches.

They ended by saying nobody knew why the diplomat had taken the high dive (they called it "leaping to his death").

Nobody asked me.

CHAPTER 2

What I remember most was the heat. It was one of those dreadful Augusts you get in Ottawa sometimes, when the temperature stays for weeks on end at a hundred (they call it thirty-five today, but that doesn't begin to tell you how hot it really is). The humidity stays at a hundred too, but it never rains. You could go through four shirts a day. If you could afford to.

It was too hot to sleep. I was already awake when I got the phone call. Someone was dead on the sidewalk in front of the Chateau Laurier. Looked like a jumper.

I skipped my morning tea, dressed as fast as I could and walked to the streetcar stop on St. Patrick Street. The streetcar let me off in front of the Chateau. I felt a quickening of blood, knowing I was at work back where I started twenty-three years ago as a young beat patrolman. I was back on Thirty Beat. Thirty Beat took in all the market area, from the Chateau Laurier to King Edward Street and from Rideau Street to the Ottawa River.

The constables had roped off the area, but that didn't stop the early morning rubberneckers from gathering. Bloody death does that to people.

In the crowd around the body was a tall man in a brown suit and a crewcut, who was flashing his badge to the constables and going pretty well where he damned well pleased. I didn't recognize him from my precinct, so I walked over.

"Busman's holiday, Mister?" I asked, polite as you please. "From out of town?"

"Sergeant Robert Carson, RCM Police." He flashed it at me, too.

Damn. Now, what did the Mounties want around here? Behind me, directly across from the canal running alongside the hotel, I could feel, rather than see, the Parliament Buildings.

"And what would the Senior Service be doing mucking about in Detective Duggan's jurisdiction, now?" I asked, putting on the blarney a bit thick, for it works better sometimes to be a dumb Mick cop.

"Pleased to meet you, Duggan," he says, putting out his hand. There was nothing for me to do but shake it. "And, as for jurisdiction, well, I guess that can be decided between the higher mucky-mucks. You know anything about this guy?"

I had just arrived. I admitted I knew less than nothing.

"His name is Walter Robinson. He's a diplomat. That's why they called me in."

I wondered who "they" were, but didn't say so. I walked over to the dead body, lifted the sheet covering Mr. Robinson. He lay crumpled into himself, like a vegetable with the juice squeezed out. There wasn't nearly as much blood as you'd expect.

I walked into the hotel. The staff were all in a dither. They didn't seem used to so many policemen around, liked to think of their hotel as a high-class place. I could tell them a thing or two.

Constables Rooney and Griffin were stationed outside the room. They let me in with a minimum of saluting and bowing. I gave them orders not to let anyone else inside. I looked out the window where he jumped. Or, as I idly thought, was pushed. I could almost reach out and touch the flag flying from the top of the Peace Tower on Parliament Hill. I could look down into the Rideau Canal. Maybe he wanted to take a swim, and dove from his window. No, not dressed right.

I straightened up and turned to find Carson at the door watching me thoughtfully.

"Rooney and Griffin don't seem to be able to follow orders too well," I remarked gently.

"An RCM Police I.D. and a pen-knife can get you into anyplace in the world," he replied, smiling.

"I'll still chew them out. For the practice."

Carson looked around, as if to memorize the room and its contents. He tried another small smile. It came out more like a grimace. "Well Duggan, I'll leave you to it for the moment. I'll go report in. I assume I'll get official jurisdiction on this case by this afternoon, maybe tomorrow. You should be glad to be out of it. In any case, it's a simple suicide, not a murder. No reason for you to get involved."

Well, now. He knew I was Homicide. Easy enough to find out, I suppose, but interesting. I walked over to the window facing Wellington Street. Since we seemed to be on a friendly last-name basis, I called him over.

"Carson, what do you see down there?"

"Nothing in particular. What do you want me to see? Just Wellington Street."

"Correct," I said, smiling. "Now, the thing is, there's a guy splattered all over that sidewalk. He's splattered all over my sidewalk, on my street. Maybe it's a suicide, maybe not. Still, that's my street. That makes it my case. Until the Chief takes me off."

He raised his hands in mock defeat. "Okay, okay. We understand each other. Official channels. I'm sure we can cooperate. No need for friction." I was starting to like him.

Griffin came inside. "There's a Mrs. Robinson would like entry to the apartment, Detective," he says, playing strictly by the book.

"Oh," says I, "I thought you just let anyone in who expressed an interest." Griffin looked hurt. Carson smiled a third time. "Okay, lad, let her in." Carson left with Griffin.

I looked again out the window. The streetcars, filled with women and children heading out to Britannia Bay for the swimming, were all slowing down for a good look. Two traffic policemen were sweating with the effort to keep the cars moving.

There were few men on the streetcars. All at work. Today, none of the young folk have ever heard of Louis St. Laurent, who was prime minister in those days, but I will say this: there was no unemployment when he ran the country. Not like today. Hell. I'm getting old.

I started a methodical review of the living room, dividing it into small squares in my mind.

Square number seven. On a table next to a chesterfield that looked too comfortable by far was a chess set. A game had been played. Black had won. The red king had been tipped over in surrender.

A slip of paper was showing from beneath the chess set. I read it. It was to the point. "Darling, it is too late for explanations. I am sorry to do this to you. Have courage. Love, Walter."

Nice guy, this Walter. From habit, I made the sign of the cross. The door opened, and I whirled around, a wee bit embarrassed to be caught in religious ritual.

Mrs. Robinson came in. Actually, she sort of glided in, like she was afraid to disturb something. Well, maybe she could.

Every generation thinks they invented sex. Today she'd be over seventy years old. If she's still alive. If somebody told you that in her youth she was about the sexiest woman on two feet, you'd probably laugh. For that matter, I like to think that I was a pretty sexy young buck in my youth. Not that you'd guess it now. My trouble was, I was raised too Catholic to really indulge myself without guilt. All the weight of the sin of lust, but none of the pleasure. Father Scanlon could tell you. But he's dead now.

She was small, but of a slimness that made her look taller. She wore an expensive shantung suit over an emerald-green blouse open at the neck. On a chain around her throat hung a single pearl. I assumed it was real. Her eyes were liquid green. Her nose was a little crooked. Her shiny dark brown hair was cut short. If each of her features was not perfect, the sum was much, much more than the total of her parts. It's funny I still remember her so vividly after all these years.

She held out a hand and locked eyes with me.

My first thought, which I admit I held too long, was that there was no way Mr. Robinson committed suicide if it meant leaving behind a wife as beautiful as Mrs. Robinson. I didn't tell her that.

"May I offer my condolences, Mrs. Robinson. Detective Duggan, Ottawa Police Force."

She didn't quite smile, but then she didn't not smile either, if you understand what I mean. "Thank you, Detective. It's been quite a shocking morning."

"I'm afraid I've got a few questions for you. Just a rough outline, we can go into more detail when you've recovered from the shock."

"I understand." She sat on a straight-backed chair, crossed her legs, and took a pink compact from her purse. She looked into the small mirror, and powdered the end of her nose. She made all that seem like a normal part of the grieving process.

The morning heat was warming up the apartment.

"Your husband left a note."

"Did he explain everything?"

"No." I handed it to her. She read it silently, folded it, handed it back. I felt sorry for her.

"Mrs. Robinson, I know this is a terrible, lonely time for you, but I must ask you a few questions. Just a few. For now."

"Yes." Just that, no other reply. She sat rigidly on the chair, her hands clutching the arms.

"Let us clear up identification first, if we might. You recognize the man on the sidewalk?"

"Walter Robinson. My husband." Her voice held no emotion.

"Perhaps you can give me his date of birth, date of marriage, biographical information."

She spoke softly for two long minutes, describing Walter Robinson's life in cold statistics, dates, numbers, names, places. I didn't interrupt her. I jotted a line or two in my notebook. It was all very official.

"Thank you, Mrs. Robinson. Now, about yourself.

"Your maiden name is?. . ."

"Martha Marie Gibson, born February 7, 1912, Bristol, England." Normally, a limey accent gives me the creeps. I can't help it, it's the way I was brought up. On her, it sounded melodic and soothing.

"You met your husband over there, Mrs. Robinson?"

"Yes, when he was studying at Cambridge."

"Cambridge, eh?"

She looked up, her eyes widening. "You sound disapproving."

I sat on the nearby chesterfield. Christ, it was getting hot! "Naw, just jealousy. I finished high school, had to start workin' the next day. No Cambridge for me." Back to official business. "Okay, when was that?"

"Nineteen thirty-five." She made it sound like yesterday. Then, she changed her mood. "About nineteen years ago. We got married in 1937."

I smiled a bit, trying to soften the next question. The least I could do. "Okay, here's the big one, Mrs. Robinson. Your husband have any reason to commit suicide that you know?"

She let the question hang in the air for a long moment.

"No."

I was a bit surprised at the finality of that answer. I tried another question. "Okay, how about any enemies that he might have had that might want to help him out the window?"

This time the answer came with no hesitation at all. "No."

I smiled because I couldn't think of anything better to do. She returned it.

I'd been a policeman for a good many years, and I knew I'd better backtrack fast. Only two questions so far. One she took too long to answer, one she answered too quick. Same answer both times. I thought I'd try it another way.

"What do you think happened to your husband, Mrs. Robinson?"

She seemed surprised at the question. She got up and moved to the mantle of the fireplace. She looked into the unlit fire, rather than at me, when she answered. "I. . .I'm not sure."

Well, if she wasn't sure, I wasn't either. "You were at home with your husband last night?"

She turned around and looked me straight in the eye. I'll give her that. "Yes. We came home around ten, we had a nightcap, and discussed a few things. Around eleven, I decided to turn in. Walter said he'd rather stay up awhile, have another drink, do some thinking. I went to bed. I fell asleep around midnight. I could hear Walter in the sitting room. When I awoke, he wasn't in bed. I wondered where he was, but thought perhaps he'd gone for an early breakfast."

"He did that often?" I really didn't care if he did or not, I just wanted to keep her talking.

"On occasion. When I went to the window, I saw and heard the commotion downstairs. I still didn't connect it with Walter, but I thought I'd have a look to see what all the fuss was."

"Did your husband have money problems?"

"No." That word again.

"Did he have a lady friend?"

She almost smiled at the delicacy of the phrase. I loosened my collar. I'd pay ten bucks for a clean, dry shirt.

"No."

We both smiled at that one. "How about you?"

"I'm a married woman, Detective." As far as that goes, when I was in England during the war I never noticed that being married ever slowed down the love affairs of English women. But I didn't say that to her. I was getting tired of the same answer all the time, however.

I tried a new tack. "Trouble at work, maybe?"

She shrugged in a sort of tired defeat. "I wouldn't know enough about it. If you've lived in Ottawa a long time, Detective, you know how secretive External Affairs can be. Even wives know so very little."

I'm a pretty straightforward guy, and this didn't seem to be going anywhere. The guy had no problems. Ergo, he didn't commit suicide. Which means somebody helped him climb out that window.

Well, let's follow that thought. "You've been in Ottawa for how long, Mrs. Robinson?"

"We left Sydney, Australia, and came here about three weeks ago."

"What made you come back to Ottawa?"

She sat next to me on the chesterfield. I pulled my tie a little tighter. "Well, Walter was getting instructions about a new posting. And there was, well, that other thing." At last.

"What thing was that, Mrs. Robinson?"

"I'm sure the people over at External can tell you more, but, well, that House Un-American Activities Committee in Washington wanted Walter to testify."

Inside, I was groaning. Complications, always complications.

Sergeant Carson was starting to make sense. "As a good guy or a bad guy?"

"What do you mean?" Her surprise at the question seemed genuine.

"I mean, to squeal on other people, or to talk about himself?"

This time she smiled thinly. I didn't get the joke. "Really, Detective, 'to squeal'? You've been reading too much lurid fiction." I was starting to like this woman. "Seriously, I don't know enough about it. Walter would never discuss the matter."

I stood up. Enough for one day. I tried a little joke. "I always thought it was okay for Canadians to engage in Un-American Activities."

She didn't laugh. If anything, her eyes were sadder. She waved her hands loosely in the air. "Oh, I'm sure it was a minor thing, about events that happened when Walter was posted in Washington during the war. He probably won't – wouldn't – have remembered anyway."

The way she threw it away like that, I was confused. "I don't get it. Your husband wasn't a communist, was he?"

She seemed surprised at the suggestion. "Oh, no. Nothing like that. If anything, Walter was a liberal. I don't even think he was socialist-leaning. Definitely not a communist."

She seemed to be getting very tired. She passed a hand across her eyes. Time to move along. "Okay, I don't think there's anything there." It might have been my imagination that I thought I saw relief soften the lines around her mouth.

I picked up my hat from the table where I had dropped it. The sweatband was serving its purpose. As I got to the door, I tried one last question. "Given all the possibilities, what do you think happened, Mrs. Robinson?"

She rose to see me out. "I'm not sure. It must have been an accident."

"He had to climb up over the sill. That's two-and-a-half feet."

She looked at me as if I had double-crossed her. Very slowly, very sadly, very softly, she said, "I honestly don't know."

I left her to her empty hotel room.

CHAPTER 3

On my way downstairs I stopped for a word or two with Rooney and Griffin. I apprised them of the fact that, in my universe, even the Mounties rated a step or two below the Lord Jesus, and when they were guarding a door against all intruders, this included Mounted Policemen. They seemed aghast at the thought that Mounties were mere humans. The follies of youth.

The details of moving the body to the morgue, as usual, took more time than you'd think. The day had been just teasing until then; now it really began to heat up. It was just going on ten a.m.

I grabbed the Number One streetcar. I figured I'd go home for a clean-up and a change before going into the station. I wished I'd put that shower in the bathroom when I wanted to. Too late now.

The Number One went up Sussex Drive to St. Patrick Street. I got off at Cobourg Street, and walked over to the house on Papineau. I still lived in the same house where I grew up, in Lowertown. Some things never change.

On the streetcar I thought about Walter Robinson. Sometimes, when you're investigating a case, a certain word or phrase pops up out of somewhere that makes the hair stand up on the back of your neck. Makes you scared that there's something there that you're not going to like. Usually, it's a word like "inheritance" or "safety deposit box" or maybe "girlfriend".

In this case, it was "House Un-American Activities Committee". Nasty people on a hysterical rampage through the garbage cans of history.

The only things I knew about American politics were what I read in the Ottawa *Citizen* newspaper and what Brother Francis-Xavier had drilled into my head in high school. But I always felt it was as full of mumbo-jumbo as any heathen nation in Africa or Asia where Brother Francis-Xavier was always collecting money to send missionaries to. The bullies, the rabble-rousers, the incredibly stupid always seemed to get to the top.

Like this senator, Joseph McCarthy, who ran the committee. Reminded me of Patrick McFadden, another Irish bully. Patrick terrorized the schoolyards of my youth. But a German bullet at Dunkirk put an end to Patrick's bullying. McCarthy was still at it. He was convinced the American administration, the state department, the army, were all riddled with communist subversives, and was using his senate committee to make the most vile, unsubstantiated charges of treason and subversion. A thoroughly scurrilous man. Yet powerful.

But how did a Canadian diplomat fit in? It didn't seem to make any sense.

If I was smart I'd use the international angle to hand all the trouble over to Carson. And nobody ever accused Pendrick Duggan of being stupid.

I bathed in cold water as best I could and changed my shirt. I needed a lighter weight jacket. The trouble was, if I bought one, with my luck it would turn cold overnight.

I wasn't surprised when I got to the station to find Carson waiting for me. He looked crisp and dry. I took it as a personal insult. My whole shirt was one huge sweat stain already.

We shook hands for the second time in one day.

"Well, Duggan, know anything you didn't know this morning?"

"Yeah. This case stinks."

"Life is cruel."

"Only the good die young."

I looked over the papers on my desk. All statistics and facts. I was supposed to make sense of it all. Robinson was forty-four, making about nine thousand a year, he was in the diplomatic corps, was on intimate terms with the minister of External Affairs and the prime minister. When I added his good-looking wife to that picture, I came up with a serious question. What makes a guy in those circumstances jump out of a seventh-storey window? Me, I don't make half that salary, I'm about the same age, I got a piece of metal in my thigh from the war, I've been a widower for eight years, you don't see me jumping from no seventh-floor window. I posed the question to Carson.

When he started to answer, I proposed that we adjourn to the Albion across the street for a couple of cold beers.

He seemed a bit incredulous. "During working hours?"

I suggested we could wait until five, but I'd rather talk right now. We crossed the street. I noticed he never wore a hat. I liked the idea.

There were a lot of policemen in the Albion, along with the usual bunch of lawyers, civil servants, informers and general hangers-on. It was a big, noisy tavern where you had to shout to make conversation. But the beer was cold and the service fast. And the temperature was slightly cooler than outside.

I thought I'd bait him right off the bat. "So, Carson, you had me thrown off this case yet?"

"Don't think I couldn't if I wanted to, Duggan." The gloves were off. I smiled. He paid the tab. Nice fellow. "Truth is," he said, lying through his teeth while he took a mouthful of beer, "I couldn't care less. It's really up to your chief and my superintendent to figure out who should be the investigator." I nodded sagely. "Thing is, there's no need for a homicide detective to investigate a suicide." He didn't meet my eyes with that line.

I finished my first draft, started on the second. "Oh, I agree with you wholeheartedly, lad." I could lie as sweetly as he could. "There's just a few strange angles that make me wonder about suicide."

He took a new track. "Suicide or not, by now you must be aware that there are international implications. Why, even the FBI might have to enter into the investigation." His eyes lit up at the mention of the FBI like Rooney's and Griffin's at the mention of the Mounties.

"Still, if I wrote it off as a suicide, and you found out different, I'd be the one lookin' the fool, now wouldn't I?" I smiled brightly.

"It's a suicide, all right." I swear I almost saw him wink.

So I tried one on him for size. "Tell you what, Carson, me boy. I'll make you a sportin' proposition. You give it to me, and I'll walk across the street and write it up as a suicide and hand it all over to you."

He sat silent for a moment, not touching his beer. A waste, I thought. "Give you what?"

I signalled the waiter for four more. "Where does that House Un-American Committee fit into this? You should know, you being a Mounted Policeman and all."

He seemed stricken that I should dare ask such a question. He leaned over confidentially, knocking over his beer in the process. I knew he would do that. The waiter was over quickly with a rag to clean up. Carson declined another. "I don't think you have enough security clearance to know that, Duggan. I'd like to tell you, really I would." His eyes beamed sincerity.

All four beers were mine now. I gulped down the second, started on the third. Thirsty work, this detecting.

I saw a lawyer I wanted to talk to. Excused myself and went over. I was back in less than a minute. The beer situation hadn't changed.

"Well, too bad. I was just looking for an excuse to hand it over to you. If I wrote a suicide report with what I know now, they'd put me back on the beat." He looked uncomfortable, as if he hated making deals. "Tell you what. Help me out. Give me a scenario I like that has this Robinson committing suicide and I'll write it up that way." He looked unconvinced. "Honest injun."

He took a tentative sip of beer, put it down quickly. He looked around as if he expected his superiors or some foreign spies to be at the next table. He made a big production of leaning confidentially across the table.

"Okay. You already know some of it. So here's the way I figure it. As you're aware, Robinson was asked to go to Washington to testify before this committee. The way I like it is Robinson was working in Washington during the war. He knew a couple of people in the British Embassy there from his Cambridge days, pretty radical guys. But he says nothing, lets them do whatever it is they were doing. Now, ten years later, the Americans want him to rat on his old college buddies. He thinks it over, death before dishonour, all that upper-class limey stuff, finds he can't do it."

"So his old Cambridge buddies were communists."

"Maybe not commies, but close enough."

"Fellow travellers."

"Yeah. Something like that." He looked distinctly uncomfortable.

I felt distinctly uncomfortable. "So he takes the high dive. You say you like it?"

He was trying to be persuasive, now. "It's clean and it's neat. And, it gives the guy some moral integrity. It's not for publication, of course, but everybody can back off. Anyway, there's no evidence of any other possibility."

He had a point. And I had to go to the bathroom.

When I got back, Carson was standing, as if to leave. I waved him into a seat. "You might have some good points there, but it's all theory and speculation." I knew that would get him going.

He bit. "There's not a shred of evidence of any foul play. And the story works."

My turn. "If there's any evidence, I'll find it."

He was irritated. "It's a goddamned suicide! Take my advice and back off right now."

I smiled. "I said if I liked your story, I'd buy it. I don't like it. The ending stinks."

He got angry or pretended to be. He stood up, yelling at me. "I knew it was a mistake to talk to you. You'll be off this case by tomorrow." He started walking away.

"Wait. Sit down one minute." Reluctantly, he turned and stood by the table. People were beginning to stare at us. "Okay, let's cut the bullshit, and I'll tell you a story. What if I change your scenario a bit, and Robinson is the commie or the fellow traveller. And the Americans are about to expose him. So, rather than face the committee, he takes the leap. Sounds better – not perfect, but better. Was Robinson a commie?" It was the second time today I'd asked that question.

Carson looked glum. He sat. "Not a chance, and I ought to know. I was part of the team investigating his background. Twice."

"Twice?"

"Normal procedure. Every few years or so diplomats get checked out, especially when they're due for a sensitive posting. He checked out clean both times. The prime minister himself vouched for him. And the minister of External Affairs."

"Yeah." I didn't meet his eyes. I meditated on my beer. I signalled for two more. It was a pain being a policeman in a capital city. Too many politicians.

Carson left the tavern without saying good-bye.

I knew it was time to get back to work, but I didn't want to walk back into that oven. I decided on two more for the road.

I walked back to my little cubbyhole to let the beer settle. I read a few reports. I put in my seventeenth request for a patrol car of my own. A detective hitching rides, taking the bus and streetcar and walking. It just wasn't fitting.

Maybe a walk would relieve the bloated feeling. At the Chateau I talked to the bell captain, the bellboys and the desk clerk. Nobody had seen or heard Robinson fall. The doorman had found his body, probably only about thirty seconds after it had landed.

The desk clerk was snotty, so I told him to come into the station later to make his statement. He complained he'd lose his pay. Serves him right.

I decided I had a new bunch of questions for Mrs. Robinson. When she let me in, I saw that she had a visitor.

Everybody in the country knows the Senator. He had been put into the senate as a reward for raising huge stacks of money for the Liberal Party. Nobody had asked any questions about where or how he found it.

He was a corpulent man, about sixty, of the sort typical in the Liberal Party forty years ago, but today found more in the Conservative Party, especially in Ontario. When he spoke, there were traces of both a French and a Scots accent. I didn't like the Senator. He was too fat and he was too powerful.

For years I had suspected him of being the epitome of corruption in politics. It really doesn't matter what party they belong to or what country they come from, there are always a handful of people who twist and corrupt the political process so that it resembles organized crime more than the art of government. I always felt the Senator could teach Al Capone a thing or two about crime. Trouble was, I had never been able to collect one shred of evidence to back up my suspicions and have him sent to jail.

We were introduced. He looked as uncomfortable as I felt.

"I came by to offer Mrs. Robinson my condolences, and to bring her up-to-date on the government action concerning the unfortunate death of her husband."

"Maybe you can bring me up-to-date as well."

"I assume, Mr. Duggan, that you're cooperating with the RCM Police on this matter..."

"More or less." I was getting tired of hearing about how it was everybody's business except mine.

"...inasmuch as it's really more in their field, a federal, perhaps even an international, matter."

"I understand."

"Well, as we all understand each other, I can tell you that this evening the P.M.'s going to get some stiff questions in the House. Of course he'll try to say as little as possible – national security and all that." The thought seemed to please him.

"I'm not surprised. What will he say about Mr. Robinson?"

The idea of answering a policeman's question pained him. "Oh, he'll defend his reputation. Vigorously, of course." He turned to Mrs. Robinson. "We, I, was wondering...of course, if there was anything in his personal life that could have led to his suicide, perhaps the political angle wouldn't even have to come into it." I enjoyed seeing him squirm.

Mrs. Robinson didn't take the hint. "I'm sure you're right," she replied. There was a long moment of silence. I turned to the window to hide the smile spreading across my face.

The Senator tried to stare her down. When that didn't work, he picked up his hat and opened the door. "Well, good day, Mrs. Robinson. I'll keep in touch. Mr. Duggan."

I figured the Senator had a whole lot more information than I did so I decided to hold on to him for awhile. "Just a second, Senator. Perhaps I could have a private word with you."

We sat across from each other in the plush lobby, people scurrying about us, some looking enquiringly at the Senator. He looked like he belonged here. I looked just like I was, a Lowertown kid out of his depth in the Chateau Laurier. I tried to get his attention right away.

"I assume you speak for the government on this case."

"Only informally, of course. We wouldn't dream of interfering with the official police investigation. . ."

"I'm sure not."

". . .by the Mounties." I had walked right into it. All I could do was smile.

"Well, until the Mounties take over, I thought I might still ask a few questions."

"I'm sure that I don't know much that can help you." He took out a stogie, lit up. Didn't offer me one. I would have refused anyway. "You don't dispute that this is a suicide, do you?" He blew smoke in my general direction.

"I don't know yet. But I had a thought. Would the government actually have let this guy go down to testify in Washington?"

"It's tricky. If I had anything to do with it, they wouldn't. If it would help bilateral relations, though, they might."

"You mean if the American government told us to do it, we would."

The Senator shook his head sadly. "You misunderstand the relationship between our two countries, Mr. Duggan."

"I bet." I was getting tired of all this pussy-footing around. "So, if he was told to go down and testify, he might have had a good reason for jumping."

"Only if he thought that was preferable to testifying." The Senator was no fool.

"What would his testimony reveal?"

We both watched a pretty girl walk by. "That's the funny part, you know. Nothing serious. It was a case of mistaken accusations. The minister even wrote to the committee putting his faith in Robinson's character. But you know these Americans. . ."

"Yeah. They're all screwy." I had met enough Americans during the war to last me a lifetime.

He stood with a look of finality, placing his hat squarely on his head. He nodded to two young women walking by. "Well, if that's everything. . ."

I stood beside him, watching them get into the elevator. "Just about. Oh, one thing. . ."

"Yes?"

"Do you know where Robinson's next posting was supposed to be?"

"I don't think it was decided yet. There were three or four possibilities – I believe Vienna, Moscow and, uh, Delhi were all mentioned. And he could have been posted right here in Ottawa, you know."

He was walking through the door held open by the doorman. I kept by his side until we were outside. It must have been over the hundred-degree mark by now. I wanted to get back inside. "Well, thanks for your time. I'll keep in touch."

The prospect didn't bring a smile to his face. "You do that." He walked away in the direction of Parliament Hill.

I still hadn't talked to Mrs. Robinson.

CHAPTER 4

I hadn't noticed earlier, but she had changed her clothes. Some widows look good in black.

"Would you come in for a cup of tea, Mr. Duggan?"

Who could refuse? "I'd love to. I was raised on tea when I was a kid. It seems more people are drinking coffee these days, but give me a hot cup of strong tea any time."

She busied herself in the tiny kitchenette. "Were you raised in Ottawa, Mr. Duggan?"

A bit of small talk wouldn't hurt. I had to raise my voice. "Yes. Right down in Lowertown. Still live in the same house where I was brought up."

"I thought Lowertown was a French area."

"Lots of French. Lots of Irish. Lots of Jews. All three being raised to hate the others."

"I'm sure you exaggerate." The kettle started whistling.

"They all hate each other until they're about fifteen. Then the Irish and the French find out that love – or sex – is a lot stronger and they all marry each other. Then, around twenty-five or so, they all go back to hating. Except for the one they married, of course."

She brought in the tea things. We sat on the chesterfield, with the tray on a little table to the side. "You sound like you married a French-Canadian." She poured.

"Yep. Not the greatest marriage. Separated for six years during the war. Then she died shortly after I came home."

"I'm sorry."

"You get used to it. You have to learn to cope alone."

"I suppose so. It will be hard."

"Yes." We were both balancing teacups. There was a long moment of silence. I'm not sure what she was thinking. I was remembering Lucille.

My beautiful Lucille. What a magical, tortured relationship we had had. She, all fire and silk. Me, all granite and steel. Oh, we had loved and hated with the best of them. I had loved her so much, yet had treated her so shabbily sometimes. Part of it was the depression, of course, and then there was the war. That damned war, which destroyed those it didn't kill.

My beautiful Lucille. I remembered the first time I had seen her, walking to church on a cool Sunday morning, the wind blowing her skirt against her legs, her hand firmly clutching her hat against her head. I remembered the last time I had seen her, her beautiful mouth hurling invectives against me.

I shook myself out of my reverie. Mrs. Robinson put her cup on the table.

"When I first met Walter, he was a student at Cambridge."

"Weren't you?"

"Oh, no. I was working in a solicitor's office. My accent is quite affected, Mr. Duggan." It was a nice accent. "No more than you could I have afforded a Cambridge education." It goes to show you how you can be fooled by an accent. "Walter was typical of many Canadians who come to study in England in that they become more British than the British themselves."

I waded in. "Foppish. Affected."

"...Well, yes, if you put it that way. Walter cut quite a dashing academic figure to a mere solicitor's assistant. He came in one day to get some legal advice on something and I was smitten.

"I'm afraid I was quite shameless in seducing him." My heart was breaking. "And so it went until he graduated and we were able to afford marriage. It was a pleasant time. I recall the many nights in my kitchen when Walter and his friends would sit around arguing politics..."

Politics seemed to be everywhere in this case. I put down my empty cup. "What kind of politics?"

She refilled the cups. She was getting positively chatty. I still hadn't asked a single question I had intended to. "Oh, every possible kind. You must understand that in those days you could argue any political cause, especially if you were a student – from nazism to communism to Sun Yat Sen-ism. It was understandable. Everyone knew that later on they would all be in government or banking or teaching at university, and then they'd all have to become good Conservatives or Liberals.

"The only politicians with no supporters at all were poor Mr. Chamberlain and Mr. Roosevelt. I'm afraid no one even considered Mr. Mackenzie King one way or the other."

She was pulling my leg. It felt all right. "I've voted for MacKenzie King many times, even organized for him. But I'm sure he wouldn't have minded if Cambridge undergraduates didn't spend all their waking hours arguing about his politics."

She got up. The window seemed to draw her and she stood looking out. "You're trying to make me smile. It's kind of you." She turned to face me. "I suppose I'll think of poor Walter a lot in the next while. I haven't stopped thinking of him all day.

"Are you a religious man, Mr. Duggan?"

I didn't have to think abut that very long. "I'm afraid so. Mass every Sunday. Confession and communion. I'm sure Father Scanlon is tired of hearing my miserable sins every Sunday. They're always the same ones – pride and lust."

She was looking out the window again. "Normal human attributes, Mr. Duggan. Not necessarily sins." Her arms were crossed tightly around her body.

"The second I don't do much about, I'm afraid. All thoughts and little action. But pride, my nemesis, haunts me every day. And takes a beating most occasions, too." I surprised myself. I wasn't used to talking aloud about my sins.

"You don't strike me as a prideful man, Mr. Duggan."

I sat silent for a long moment. I would have liked to tell her to call me Pen, but it didn't seem very professional to do so. This definitely wasn't turning out to be the interview I had in mind. What the hell.

"Well, I'm afraid you misread me, Mrs. Robinson." I rather

liked the idea of calling her Martha, but that didn't seem professional either. "It's my downfall all the time." At last, I saw a way to get back on track. "And I must say, in a selfish way, that your husband's death is hurting my pride."

"How so?"

"Well, I come over here to check on an apparent suicide. But, after I've been here awhile, I'm no closer to figuring out what happened this morning or why. If anything, I know less now than when I came over this morning. Everything just seems to be going around in circles."

She sounded thoughtful. "It might be more straightforward than you think."

That sounded good, but I was doubtful. "Maybe. When I was a patrolman, they gave me my own neighbourhood, you know, Lowertown, to look after. And I was good.

"They were my own streets where I was born and bred. And I kept them clean. As clean as I could.

"That's why I was promoted. I had a knack for knowing when someone was telling the truth, or when something didn't look right. So I was promoted to Burglary. Then Vice.

"I wasn't any good at Vice. Too rough on people. I wouldn't allow them on my territory. I just moved them somewhere else where the policeman was easier than me. Hell, there's no detective work in Vice.

"Anyway, continue the story. You got married. No kids?"

"No. Walter is – was – not the most lustful of men. Unlike you." I could feel the shirt sticking to my back. "He was. . . fastidious. We had an ordered – a sophisticated, modern – marriage. And children didn't fit in. After a few years, even my own ardour was diminished."

I thought I could begin to like her, and told her so.

"I'm sure you could, Mr. Duggan. As soon as you stop thinking that I might have thrown my husband out of that window."

She was full of surprises. "I thought no such thing."

"Nonsense. You're more transparent than you think."

She had me all right. No doubt my thoughts were evil. "Well, I just don't like you being in the bedroom asleep when your husband commits suicide. It just doesn't seem right."

"As in 'fitting'?"

"Yeah. It's a nasty thing to do to your wife, if that's the way it happened. Was he a nasty man?"

"No more than most men."

I deserved that. But I persevered. "Did he have any visitors last night?"

She paused. She looked into my eyes. I looked away. "No. At least, not that I know. I told you I fell asleep."

Argh. Let the Mounties figure it out. "Okay. I'm convinced. Your husband committed suicide while of unsound mind. He was depressed and worried about testifying in Washington. That's enough for now. Thanks for the tea. Don't get up, I'll see myself out. See you later."

I had some thinking to do.

I went down to the lobby, told the desk clerk to be at the station in an hour to give his statement. Then I phoned the station and told them I couldn't make it, to take the guy's statement and let him go. The hell with him.

I took the streetcar home. Going up St. Patrick Street, the trolley passed St. Brigid's Church. On impulse, I jumped off.

Father Scanlon was in the rectory.

"Got a cold one, Father?"

"You know the only thing I have is brandy, my boy." Father Scanlon drank sinfully expensive brandy. His predecessor, Father Bradley, was a hopeless drunk, so Father Scanlon kept to a few brandies a day, the better to avoid scandal.

"Well, better that than nothing, I suppose. Mind you, I come over often enough that you could keep a few beer in the ice box for the occasional visit."

"Wouldn't do, my boy. Wouldn't do. I'd have visits from all the riff-raff of the parish if they knew I kept beer in the ice box."

Brandy is okay if you intend to drink the whole bottle. This drinking from snifters and holding to only one or two defeats the purpose. But it was nice to talk to someone who wasn't going to tell me I had no business doing what I was doing.

Father Scanlon had heard my confession so often, he knew me better than my own mother. Even so, the odd time I committed sins so disgusting they would strain our friendship, I walked over to St. Joseph's parish to relieve my guilt.

"That was a lazy sermon you gave Sunday. I heard most of it before. Had a hangover, Father?"

"No such thing. A good sermon bears repeating. People continue doing the same thing anyway."

"That's for true, Father. That's for true."

"And what did you think of my telling those frogs to go to their own church on Sunday? I'm thinking of cancelling the noon Mass. Just because those Frenchies like to sleep in of a Sunday doesn't mean they should come into my parish. And Ste. Anne's just a few blocks away. Oh, I've talked to the Monsignor about it. Told him to have his own noon Mass, keep his parishioners where they belong."

I liked Father Scanlon, but you'd never know we all belonged to the same church. "Well, I like to sleep in the odd time myself, Father. Tell you the truth, if it was Ste. Anne's had the noon Mass instead of St. Brigid's, I guess I'd go to Ste. Anne's myself."

"You wouldn't!" He sounded properly scandalized. "Here, have another, and banish such evil thoughts from your head. Ste. Anne's, indeed!" I had opened a touchy subject.

"Thank you, Father. It's going to be a long day. I'm going to change, then get back to work."

"Thank the Lord for the boys in blue." Father Scanlon had seen too many Pat O'Brien movies.

"So, tell me, Father, any news?" Sometimes, it's nice to hear about regular people doing regular things, instead of death and robbery and assault all the time.

"Well, you probably haven't noticed, but Mrs. Mallory is expecting again."

"Again? How can they afford it?"

"Pendrick, it's almost a sin to think that way. The Good Lord will provide."

"Well, just so long as Mr. Mallory isn't expected to."

"Perhaps he can ask for a raise. Mind you, that Jew he works for will probably turn him down. Well, I guess they'll just have to tighten their belts a little." Irish Catholics were the only people who counted to Father Scanlon.

"The patrolman was telling me that the oldest Mallory – I forget his name – Larry, or something. . ."

"Terry."

"That's it, Terry. Anyway, he's starting to get into a bit of trouble. He's left alone to wander the streets too much. Another baby is all they need."

"That's the way of the world, Pendrick." I think Father Scanlon liked the sound of the name Pendrick because it sounded so Celtic. When I was a boy, I had a fight a day, regular as clockwork, over that name.

"One comes into the world just as one goes into jail. If that's the way of the world, it's a cruel world, for sure."

"Well, I'll tell you. It's those socialist Liberals of yours who cause all the trouble. Then they try to solve the problems they've caused. Now, take that Family Allowance they've introduced. I might be against it myself, but at least it will help the Mallory family."

I thought I'd best leave the subject of the socialist Liberals alone. The one bitter fight the two of us had ever had was when Father Scanlon used his pulpit to imply to the parish that it was a sin to vote Liberal. And me a Liberal all my life and my parents before. I told him if he ever did it again, I'd leave the parish and go to Ste. Anne's, and take as many families with me as I could. Since Lowertown always voted at least ninety per cent Liberal, it was no idle threat.

Now the wily old priest was more subtle. He put the word "liberal" in quotations dripping with sarcasm as he railed against all forms of modernist thinking and sinning. When Louis St. Laurent was elected prime minister, I thought I had him, pointing out we had a good Catholic prime minister. He wasn't convinced. "Ah, but he's a French Catholic, my boy. Not the same thing. Not the same thing at all."

But, for all that, he had a head on his shoulders. I thought I'd pick his brains a bit. "Heard anything about that death up at the Chateau Laurier, Father?"

"Just the newscast. Suicide. Not a Catholic." As if Catholics never committed suicide.

"It's my latest case."

"Well, that means it's probably a murder, not suicide. Good, good. Suicide's a sin."

"And murder's not?"

"Not the same thing at all. In suicide, the victim and the perpetrator are the same person. It's the perpetrator, not the victim, who's the sinner."

"I see your point. Well, tell me this then, Father. Now, I know you can't bury a suicide victim in a Catholic cemetery. Well, why not? The victim's committed no sin. Maybe you shouldn't bury the perpetrator, as you call it, but why not bury the victim?"

Sometimes it was easy to confuse Father Scanlon, and he would try to bluff his way out. "Ah, Pendrick, I wish I had time to explain to you. But, without the training of years in the seminary, I'm afraid I could never get the subtleties through your thick Irish head."

"Father, seriously, now." He looked aggrieved that I hadn't taken his answer seriously. "You take a young man, all the prospects in the world, a good-looking wife, maybe just a hint of scandal in his background, but easily overcome, why do you think he would commit suicide?"

"No faith, my son. No faith."

"What kind of an answer is that?"

"As vague as the question you put to me."

"My head will burst over this one."

"What little you've told me and I heard it on the radio leads me to doubt suicide. But then, it could be just the way you phrased the question. It could be you don't want it to be suicide. Then you'd be out of a job."

He could be right, of course.

I left him, grabbed a bite to eat at Imbro's Italian restaurant on Rideau Street, and went on home. I made a few phone calls, had the last beer in the ice box, read the paper, took another bath, and put on my third shirt of the day. I kept the same tie.

The radio said it was going down to eighty-five overnight.

I took another streetcar. I got off on Wellington Street in front of Parliament Hill. I went into the visitor's gallery to listen to the evening question period. Maybe the opposition had better questions to pose than I did.

Everything went as planned by the Senator. The opposition asked a few soft questions. The prime minister railed at the McCarthy witch-hunt destroying a brilliant career. He swore Robinson was Jesus Christ in pinstripe. A woman sitting near me in the visitor's gallery whispered that the only good commie was a dead one. At least she didn't have any doubts. I wondered who she was.

I decided to walk at least part way home. I was half-convinced that Mrs. Robinson had pushed her husband out the window. Or at least didn't try to stop him.

Too bad. I rather liked her.

CHAPTER 5

I suppose I shouldn't have bought a case of beer from Aurèle Lemieux. It's probably both a sin and a dereliction of duty to frequent a bootlegger. But it was hot.

When I walked into the house, the phone was ringing. I got it on about the tenth ring. It was a lady.

"This is Detective Duggan?" Whoever it was, she had a foreign accent.

"The same."

"You are investigating the death of Walter Robinson?" I admitted I was.

"If you would meet me tomorrow morning, I could give you some information perhaps." At last. Someone actually volunteering information.

"Where?"

"Let us say Strathcona Park."

"When?"

"At eight a.m. I will be by the fountain." She hung up. I had said six words.

The shirt went into the laundry hamper. The first beer went down my throat. I leafed through *Liberty* magazine.

I was restless. It was too hot to sleep. The next beer went down nice and easy. I sat on the front porch, in my undershirt, watching the kids play in the street. It was too hot for them to sleep, too. There was all of Anglesea Square to play in, but they had to play in the streets. Same as I did when I was a kid.

Old Joe Lepage from across the street came over to chat. I got a few more from the ice box. Joe was a retired sheet metal worker. He had been a strong union organizer. We discussed a strike on a construction site in Mechanicsville. We agreed it might turn violent soon.

"A couple of us old retired ones from this local went over to walk the picket line with them yesterday. My wife gave me hell for sticking my nose in where it don't belong.

"She was right. They didn't know us. Didn't welcome us. Ah, these young workers today. I don't even know what they are striking for half the time. In my day, we knew what a strike was all about: money. Money and pensions.

"You know, Mr. Duggan, for a policeman, you're not too bad." I had just given him a second beer. "When I was in the union, I got beat up by so many policemen, I thought I hated them all. But you're an exception."

"Thanks, Joe."

"Sometimes, before the war, I'd come home, my head all bleeding from the beatings I took, and I'd see you walking the beat in your uniform, and I'd think to myself, 'Now, there's a fine young man; if they asked Constable Duggan to help break up a strike, he'd probably refuse'."

Well, he was wrong there, but I didn't tell him. He was a good neighbour, even if he did hate all policemen. Except me, of course.

After we had analyzed the next day's weather thoroughly, I went inside. No use even getting undressed. The house was even hotter than the streets. It smelled musty and old. It gave me a depressed feeling.

Maybe it didn't make any sense for one man to live in a whole house. They had put up a lot of new apartment buildings since the war. Maybe I should move into a nice one-bedroom apartment, closer to the station.

Hell. It was the heat. No wonder people committed suicide, weather like this.

I decided to take a walk. I put on a short-sleeved shirt. The fourth one today, I thought as I locked the door.

Memories. When I was a kid. Down Papineau. Across Anglesea

Square (which was always called Angel Square by all the Irish kids), past York Street School, then over to St. Patrick. Up to Dalhousie. I was back on Thirty Beat. Couldn't help myself: told a few girls on Dalhousie to move along. Walked up to George Street, then over to King Edward. Past the synagogue.

I had tried so hard to keep those streets clean. But I could see the poverty, the hopelessness. The boys and girls, they just want to get out. And they can't. They all got jitterbug fever. I had a few ideas as I walked.

A couple of hoods looked like they wanted to jump me, so I went over and slapped some sense into them. I'm getting too old. I got no patience.

But, I was thinking. The more I thought, the more I wanted to take a bomb and just blow up this neighbourhood. I could see it so different. Nice, with pretty houses, flowers in the windows.

Would people be any happier if I blew it up? I doubted it. Maybe someone else would do it for me.

Three of the Savageau sisters were sitting on their porch, flirting with the young men who walked by. In the neighbourhood, we knew them as the Savage sisters – seven of them. The name fit. Everybody knew the Savage sisters, and every young man claimed to have slept with at least three of them. If all the stories were true, the poor girls wouldn't have had time to do anything else.

I chatted them up a bit, but their attention wandered. I was too old for them. My mother would have described them as being no better than they had to be. I thought maybe they were better than they could have been.

I had one last beer as a nightcap. I relieved myself. The pipes rattled when I flushed. Another expense coming up soon.

I slept on top of the bedding, tossing and turning in the heat. I woke several times. My dreams were a mess. Mrs. Robinson. A girl in a park. The war. Gunfire. A dead man on a wet street in Paris. Lucille in a green silk dress, taunting me.

In my dreams, I relived my courtship of Lucille, me in my police uniform, she in her green silk dress. I chased her in a passion, but she was so far ahead. Every once in awhile, she would stop on a street corner and wait for me to get closer. Then she would run again, laughing and smiling and winking at all the men on the street. I yelled at her in French, but she wouldn't reply, she just kept running and laughing. Finally, with a desperate lunge, I caught her and we fell tumbling to the ground. I woke up then, my body covered with the effort of running. Or dreaming.

I got up and tried to sleep in an easy chair in the living room. Too uncomfortable to dream. Or to sleep.

I was up before the sun. I put the kettle on to boil while I dressed. They said that hot tea was better than a cold drink in weather like this. I hoped so.

When I was irritable like I was this morning, things usually happened. I was in a mood to cause trouble. Just to stir things up and see what jumped. Maybe the Chief would pull me off the case today. I better cause some trouble fast.

In the event, I didn't have to do anything. I walked up to Wurtemburg Street, then down to Charlotte, and up Charlotte to Laurier. I figured I'd get there about a half-hour early, just to look around.

I was just coming around the corner onto Laurier, past the Russian Embassy, when I saw the flashing light and the people gathered around the fountain.

"We tried to call you, Detective, but there was no one at home." The patrolman looked all of eighteen.

"I was walking in this morning."

"This man found the girl." I looked over to see a balding civil-servant type, briefcase still in hand. I was surprised he had taken the time to call the police and stay around.

I ignored him for the moment, and looked down at the dead girl. The back of her head had been bashed in. Her eyes stared into the sky.

I straightened up. Unbidden thoughts filled my head. "Have you called the ambulance yet?" As I spoke, the ambulance pulled up, and the patrolman pointed.

"Okay. Move fast. Get the body into the morgue right now. Make it a Jane Doe, even if you find any identification."

"We couldn't find any, Detective."

"Good. Get going. When you get back to the station, write me up a report, put it on my desk in a sealed envelope. No copies.

"Don't answer any questions from anybody about this. That means the press, the Mounties, the Chief. Nobody. Refer everybody to me." He looked confused. "Do this right and there'll be a citation for you." He beamed, and began issuing orders sternly. Good lad.

I needed time to think. Now they could take me off the Robinson case, and I could still do some work. I assumed this was the same girl who had called me last night. I looked at my watch: seven forty-five. If it wasn't the same girl, the right one would be here in fifteen minutes.

By ten of eight, everybody was gone, except the civil servant. He looked worried. He was probably due in the office in ten minutes. I took his name, address and phone number. He worked for the immigration department.

I shooed him away, and told him I'd contact him later for a statement. If there was a book, I sure wasn't playing by the rules in it.

I sat on the fountain until eight-thirty. No young lady showed. I had a murder on my hands. Good.

I stood and gazed across the park. From where I stood, near Laurier Avenue, the ground took a sudden dip, leading down towards the river. Far away in the distance, Dutchy's swimming hole was welcoming the first bathers of the day. A train crossed the old black railroad bridge next to the abattoir. The acres of grass and trees were separated from the river by a footpath. Nobody was walking along the footpath.

I walked down the steps leading towards the river, counting them as I descended. There were sixty-one. I wandered down to the river and walked along, my hands clasped behind my back.

The funny thing was, this meant a murder and a suicide, or maybe even two murders, in two days. In Ottawa. Now, Ottawa just wasn't the sort of town that had a murder a day. Months went by without one. Things were so slow that I wasn't even full-time on Homicide. We didn't have such a department.

I threw a few rocks into the river, watching them skip across. I wasn't as good at it as I had been as a kid.

A little girl stood on the grass, watching me. "Get to school, kid," I growled. She ran away in terror.

I crossed the park and climbed up back to the fountain. I searched the grass for anything I might find. Nothing.

I walked up Laurier towards the station. After two blocks, I took off my jacket and slung it over my shoulder. This morning, I had been smart. I carried a spare shirt in a paper bag. It would be crumpled when I put it on. Maybe no one would notice.

I walked past Laurier House, where Mackenzie King used to live when he was prime minister. I remembered seeing him walk his dog along this street many's the time before he died.

They say he used to talk to ghosts. Still and all, he was a good Liberal.

When I got to the station, I went into the morgue to look at my Jane Doe. At least it was cool there.

She looked to be about thirty. Nice enough looking in life, I supposed. Her hair was shorter than the normal. They had taken off her clothes. I wasn't aroused.

I had a sudden thought to make sure the coroner took special notice of her dental work and any operations she might have had in her life. You never know.

Funny she didn't have a purse. Maybe whoever bashed her took it with him.

I shook my head vigorously. Somehow the image of Lucille, lying in the same morgue eight years ago, had entered my thoughts. I didn't like the picture.

I left there fast. The coolness had been nice, though.

I went up to Missing Persons. That wasn't a whole department either, just a clerk and a part-time officer. Ottawa was a pretty steadfast town. Not too many people went missing unless they wanted to.

"I want to see any files on women, twenty-five to thirty-five, reported missing in the last three weeks." I had no idea what I was looking for.

I looked through her clothes. Her skirt had a Montreal label, but all the rest were national brands.

Lots of women did their shopping in Montreal. They had the

latest Paris fashions in Montreal. All guaranteed to make even the prettiest woman look foolish.

I hate the waiting. I like to be out and about. But I had to wait for the constable's report, the coroner's report, all the paperwork.

The Mounties couldn't take this away from me now.

The phone didn't stop ringing all morning. The first call came in when I was going over the desk clerk's statement from the day before. It seemed straightforward enough to me, but there was a small thought nagging at me that I couldn't get straight in my mind.

It was the Chief on the phone. We had a meeting with a Superintendent Francis of the Mounties at two o'clock this afternoon.

"We are going to cooperate aren't we, Duggan?" There was a hint of mild threat in the question.

"Whatever you order me to do, Chief."

"By the sweet Lord Jesus, Duggan, it's not what I order, it's what's right." The Chief liked to swear like an Irishman when he talked to a Mick policeman.

"The only thing is, I worry about them trying to cover things up. The victim is a friend of the prime minister."

He yelped. "The prime minister! Then, for the sweet love of Jesus give them everything you've got. I don't need that kind of trouble. Bring your files along with you." He hung up without saying goodbye.

I happen to have a total recall memory for conversations. It's a gift. I never keep notes, so the file was empty. I figured I better write a few things, just for appearances.

When I was a rookie constable I never wrote in my notebook until one day in court a bright lawyer convinced the judge I couldn't possibly have remembered the circumstances that precisely. After that, I jotted a few notes just before entering the courtroom.

The process of justice mystified me when I was a rookie. I knew that all policemen lied on the witness stand all the time. That was all right, because all the accused lied all the time as well.

In those days I used to confess to lying on the witness stand to old Father Bradley. This was before Father Scanlon's time. One day at confession, he asked me to meet him in the rectory.

"Duggan, I've got to talk to you. You don't seem to get the hang of this confession stuff. You're supposed to promise not to commit the sin again, but every week you come back and admit to lying on the witness stand.

"Now, there's at least a dozen other policemen in this parish, and not a one of them ever confesses to lying under oath. Are you the only policeman who does it?"

"Well, Father, I wouldn't want to speak for the others, but I suspect if we all told the truth, nobody would ever go to jail." He looked rather worried. "But it's all right, Father, all the witnesses lie, too. The judge just has to believe our lies better than theirs."

"Duggan, perhaps you're over-zealous on this matter. Maybe it's just a question of interpretation of the truth."

"That's it, Father. Perhaps you could give a sermon on Sunday about the nature of truth. And point out that it's a sin to lie under oath."

"Duggan, you misunderstand me!" He banged his big fist on the rectory table. "I don't want all the others confessing, I want you to stop."

"I could try to tell more of the truth, Father, but even the judges won't like it."

Father Bradley had a sudden shrewd thought. "Now, what is it you swear your oath on, Duggan?"

"The bible."

"No, no. I mean, what bible?"

"What bible? I don't know. King James, I suppose."

"Ah, that's it then, my boy. That's the Protestant bible. No sin at all. Well, maybe a small venial sin. Not a proper Catholic bible. No need to confess the sin at all." The matter was settled for him.

I continued confessing to lying on the witness stand until Father Bradley was gone. When Father Scanlon replaced him, I stopped. It wasn't as much fun anymore.

I wrote up a synopsis of my two meetings with Mrs. Robinson, the hotel staff and the Senator. I added the autopsy report and the statement from the desk clerk. I wrote nothing about the body in the park.

My sister-in-law called to remind me of my brother's birthday next week.

A lawyer called to remind me of a court case coming up on Friday. A waste of time. I'd go and lie my head off.

Missing Persons called to say they had my files ready. I went up and got them. Seven women reported missing in the last few weeks. More than I would have thought. Maybe I wasn't keeping tabs on things as well as I used to.

While I was gone, I had a call from the assistant deputy minister of External Affairs. When I returned his call, he was at a meeting.

Finally it was noon, and I could go over to the Albion. I had two hours to drink and think before the meeting.

It was crowded. I finally spotted a table where I could sit alone. I raised my first glass to the young lady in the park. May her soul rest in peace.

CHAPTER 6

The meeting wasn't so bad. Superintendent Francis of the RCM Police was a big man, even bigger than my six-foot-one, but with a softness from too many years behind a desk. He needed to get out on the streets more.

He was smooth. A result, no doubt, of years of wheeling and dealing with lawyers, judges, politicians and other police forces. The way he described the deal, the Mounties would take the lead in investigation, but would keep us informed and involved at all stages. It sounded too good to be true. It probably was.

I figured I'd pull his leg a bit. "Well, Chief, does that mean I should cancel those airline flights to Washington?"

Superintendent Francis's eyes grew wide as he blustered. "I really can't see any circumstances where..." He caught himself and flipped his statement inside out. "...You can see that is the exact kind of circumstance where we could do the investigating much easier, inasmuch as we already have officers stationed at the embassy in Washington."

The Chief sat silently behind his desk. Sometimes he had an operating sense of humour. He let me bait Francis. "Security staff," I scoffed.

"Security in more ways than one, Detective. More ways than one." He let the other ways hang mysteriously in the air.

I guess the Chief figured things had gone far enough. "It's settled, then. We'll let you take the lead in this thing, and provide support where needed." Francis smiled agreeably.

I stalled for a bit, out of habit. "Fine with me. I'll just put all the results so far into a file and hand it over to you, say at this time tomorrow afternoon."

Francis looked shocked. "Tomorrow? I rather thought we could just get it over with right now."

"Well, we're a wee bit short-staffed right now, what with summer holidays and all. I could work on the file this evening and tomorrow morning."

There wasn't much he could do except agree. We all shook hands.

The Chief asked me to stay around for a minute. "You've got the file in your hands. Why not just give it to him? What devilish plan are you cooking up in that devious mind, Duggan?"

"It's nothing, Chief. Nothing at all. I just thought I'd give us an extra day to work on things. If I figured everything out by tomorrow, we wouldn't have to hand anything over. And if I solved the whole thing, why of course I'd give you all the credit, say it was you who pointed me in the right direction."

"Flatterer. Toady. Seducer. You'll be my downfall yet. I don't know why I listen to you. Tomorrow. Two p.m. Hand it over. All of it."

"Yes, sir. Whatever you say."

I left. I had twenty-four hours to roam the streets and figure things out. Not much time.

I went down to look through the missing persons files. A suicide, a murder, seven missing women, all on my desk in one day. What was this city coming to? Twenty years ago, all of the illegal action was across the bridge, over in Hull, Quebec. Ottawa had always been a quiet city. Maybe a few houses of ill repute, a few gambling dens, a couple of after-hours drinking joints. All the really bad things were done by the politicians up on the Hill, but mostly done legally or connived to appear legal. It used to be you could keep the lid on things.

Maybe it was the war changed everything. I don't know. But I don't like it.

Every single woman who had gone missing had a different story. None of them was the girl in the park. I figured if I had a week to work full-time, I could find five of the women. They had just walked out, to try to start over again, probably with another man. When they wanted to, they'd show up again. Probably best to let them be for the time being.

Hell. What were women coming to these days? Then I thought of Lucille, and guessed they hadn't changed all that much. I thanked the Lord my poor sainted mother was gone. She never would have understood.

My mother never did understand Lucille. To her, Lucille was just another working-class French girl from Lowertown, the kind who led good Irish boys astray. All around her, she saw good Irish boys being led astray, and she sternly disapproved.

I guess my mother was out of her time; she would have fit in perfectly well in a small nineteenth-century Irish village. She had borne two healthy sons, miscarried another son and two daughters, and had a son and a daughter stillborn. She then considered her duty to God and her husband complete. Her only remaining tasks in life were to keep her house spotlessly tidy and to somehow put three meals on the table each day.

Lucille never understood my mother, either. Sometimes, with a giggle, she would invite me to imagine my mother and father in bed. The thought drove her to earthy laughter. It only made me angry. The angrier I got, the more Lucille would laugh. Finally, her imagination would drive us to passion, or to blows.

I guess that was the essence of Lucille and me. Passion and blows. Maybe Lucille was driven too much by passion, and I was driven too much by blows. Anyway, she's long gone now, and my mother never would have understood.

The patrolman came by with his report on the dead woman in the park. He was all spit and polish. Bucking for a promotion. I didn't tell him that my recommendations for promotions were all overruled. I guess the Chief figured that if I recommended somebody, it meant he was a loner, a troublemaker, and an all-round pain in the ass.

They had canvassed all the houses in the neighbourhood. Nobody had seen or heard anything. Somebody bashes in a girl's skull in a city park, and nobody sees or hears anything.

Two images filled my head. In the first, I was looking down at a dead man facing away from the Houses of Parliament. In the second, I was looking down at a dead woman facing away from the Russian Embassy.

I felt like someone was walking over my grave.

Well, the first thing to do was find out who the woman was. I asked for a bunch of photos to be made up of her dead face. "As pretty as possible." I rounded up four patrolmen to make the rounds of all the boarding houses, rooming houses and hotels. The first step. Four men weren't enough, but it was all I could find.

I tried to return the phone call from the assistant deputy minister of External Affairs again, but he was still in a meeting. If I knew anything, the meeting was probably about how to foil the efforts of law enforcement agencies to find out any of their grimy little secrets.

To hell with him. I'd come by his house tonight. Shake up his comfy Alta Vista home a bit. The thought pleased me.

I sat and mused about what I knew so far. I laughed aloud, startling the other officers around, at the thought that probably everyone wanted me to think Robinson committed suicide because it was true.

What I had said to Carson was also true. If Robinson was really a commie in his youth and was about to be unmasked, I'd have no trouble believing he committed suicide. That's the difference between the upper classes and the kids from Lowertown. Nobody could ever blackmail any of us over what we had ever done, because we really didn't care if everybody knew about our indiscretions. Because I had been raised as a good Irish kid to hate the Brits so much, I had become very close to being a Nazi sympathizer in my youth. That neither stopped me from spending six years of my life fighting them nor would I be embarrassed to admit it today. To tell the truth, I wasn't the only Canadian who had, at first, thought Hitler wasn't so bad.

My musings were cut short by a phone call from the Senator. It seemed he had some information for me, and could I drop by in an hour or so? I could.

I checked with a few of the others sitting around the precinct. The temperature hadn't quite hit a hundred today yet. Positively a cool spell. I changed my shirt, and decided to walk to the senate.

A tough-looking spinster secretary led me into the spacious office. The Senator called her Constance, pronouncing it in the French manner. He dismissed her, then rose from behind his huge desk and motioned us over to a settee. He poured drinks from a hidden bar. It wasn't hidden because he wasn't supposed to drink in his office, just because of the aesthetics.

"I've just come from a meeting with the P.M." I was suitably impressed. "He wants you to know how much we appreciate your hard work in this matter." I bet.

"I always vote Liberal, not to worry."

"By God, Duggan, if you had ever worked for me, we'd rule the world by now." I knew enough about the Senator to know I'd never work for him in any circumstances, but I held my tongue. "Imagine not being impressed by the thought that the P.M. was just talking about you."

"I'm impressed. I just don't like showing it."

"I understand all is roses between your force and the RCM Police. Good feelings all around."

"We're cooperating."

"Good, good." He refilled my glass. He hadn't touched his yet. "I had rather hoped Sergeant Carson could join us today, but he's been unfortunately detained." I could live with that. "The reason I asked you here was to ask you where your investigation stood at the moment."

"I thought you said you had some new information for me."

"Oh, that. Well, I had expected Sergeant Carson to be here. I'm afraid I can't really divulge anything without his presence."

The senatorial runaround.

I drained my second glass. This time, he made no move to refill it. I figured I'd better play his game so I could get out of there as soon as possible.

"I don't know a lot more than I knew yesterday. Robinson either fell or was pushed from his hotel window. His wife was either asleep or she pushed him. He either had some late-night visitors or he didn't. He either was a commie or he wasn't. He either was afraid to testify in Washington or he wasn't. Lots of either-or choices."

"If that's as far as your investigation has taken you, I don't wonder that you're glad to hand it over to the RCM Police." He was being insulting now. I figured I wouldn't get a refill, so I stood to leave.

"Senator, I walked a long way in this god-awful heat to talk to you. So far as I can tell, it's been a waste of both our time."

There was a small knock on the door, and another fellow walked in. He was a short, slim lad in shirt-sleeves and a bow tie. He waved at the Senator and smiled at me.

"I hope I'm not too late."

The Senator came from behind his desk. "Not at all. Mike, I'd like you to meet Detective Pendrick Duggan of the local police force." He emphasized the word 'local.' "Duggan, this is Mike Pearson, secretary of state for External Affairs."

We shook hands and exchanged dishonest pleasantries about how pleased were were to meet each other.

I was impressed. A minister in the flesh. Maybe now I'd get some answers. The Senator rubbed his hands together briskly and launched into things. He offered Pearson a drink, which was politely declined. He didn't offer me another one.

"Detective Duggan is in charge of the investigation into the unfortunate suicide of Walter Robinson," the Senator began. I looked into Pearson's eyes. They betrayed nothing. He benignly returned my glance, sitting on the edge of the Senator's desk.

"Robinson was a good man," he ventured. "Sound ideas. Good diplomat. He represented Canada well." He had a bit of a lisp when he talked.

I followed his train of thought. "Doesn't sound like a man who'd commit suicide."

Pearson jumped down from the desk, rubbing his hands along his trousers. "Drove him to it."

"Who did?"

"American right-wingers. To those guys, if you don't believe in lynching Negroes, killing Russians and beating your wife, you're a bloody commie. Makes it hard to be diplomatic when you're dealing with them. I'm always diplomatic, though." He smiled broadly. I was sure he was right.

"What about some other cause of death? Have you ever considered the possibility that he might not have committed suicide?"

"Any evidence of that?"

"No evidence one way or the other."

"They drove him to it." The matter was settled for him. "Thank God none of their ilk will ever get into power in Washington. Still cause trouble, though."

I decided to try the famous all-purpose question. "Are they right? Was Robinson a commie?"

The Senator glared at me. Pearson laughed.

"About as communist as you are, Detective."

I tried a joke. "That answer solves nothing. If we had a labour party here, like they do in England, I'd probably vote for them. That would make me a commie in many eyes."

"Not in mine, Detective." Pearson came close and stared into my eyes. I could see why he could be a good diplomat. "Let me put it this way: Robinson was not a communist, he was not a subversive, not a traitor. I, personally, will defend him in private and in public." His eyes, staring deep into mine, dared me to disbelieve him.

"You're saying he was being falsely accused, and he couldn't take the pressure. So he jumped."

"Sounds logical to me." Abruptly, Pearson put his hand out to me. I shook it. With a half-wave, he was out the door.

The Senator came to walk me out. "Good man, Pearson. Be a senator someday." He made that sound like a big deal. It didn't sound so great to me.

Constance led me through the echoing corridors towards the real world. Pearson hadn't said much, but he said it with great finality. One thing for sure: I certainly knew what the official line was. I squared my hat on my head and took a deep breath.

When I walked out onto the Hill, the heat slammed against me. A cold drink or a hot tea seemed in order.

I had probably drunk enough beer for one afternoon. The nearest maker of hot tea I knew was Mrs. Robinson.

I was informed that Mrs. Robinson had left the hotel in the company of a Mountie with a crew cut. Oh, great. I'm wasting my time with the Senator and Carson is walking off with the grieving widow.

With every step I took towards the station, sweat dripping from my armpits, down my arm, splashing off my forehead, my anger was growing until it was a red hot ball of fire ready to explode at the first person who stood in my way. If somebody had accidentally bumped against me on the street, he would have ended up in hospital.

I marched into the station, slamming doors behind me. People looked at me out of the corner of their eyes, but no one made a move to talk to me.

There were several new reports on my desk, but I was too angry to read them.

To hell with tea. I jammed my hat on and strode over to the Albion.

And to hell with beer. I ordered the good Irish. Doubles. I threw two of them down my throat. My anger evaporated slowly. Then I ordered four drafts. My jacket, tie and hat lay on the chair opposite me. I figured I was in fighting trim. The trouble was, I had no one to fight against.

Detective Brunowski sauntered over and sat down, shifting my clothes to another chair. I always liked Brunowski. He had been given a job on the force because he used to play for the Ottawa Rough Riders football team and that was part of the deal. Either that or the fire department. But Brunowski had fooled them all and become a good investigator. He had to, because when his playing days were over there was no way they would have kept a polack on the force if he hadn't been good.

"Duggan, how's she goin'?"

"Not so great." I brought him more or less up to date.

"Ah, ya don't solve no cases sittin' here, Duggan."

"Tell ya the truth, Bruno, I think I solved more sittin' here than anywhere else."

"Yeah. I'm goin' over to the club. Wanna come spar a coupla rounds?"

"Too hot, Bruno."

"Ah, ya sweatin' anyway. Might's well get a good workout. Then a nice, cold shower. Make the world of difference."

"I'll walk you over. That's enough of a workout for me. Maybe you got some bright ideas for me."

As we crossed the Laurier bridge, Bruno snapped his fingers of a sudden. "You remember that Gouzenko case?"

I was still overseas when that happened. "Not too much. Russian spy who defected, wasn't he?"

"A cipher clerk. Walked right into one of the local newspapers, I think it was the *Journal*, with a bunch of secret papers. They gave him the bum's rush. End of '45, I think it was."

"What about him?"

"Well, I was thinking. See, he had a whole list of all the Canadians who were helping the commies spy on us. Even a member of parliament.

"What I was thinking was, if this diplomat of yours was really a commie spy, Gouzenko woulda turned him over, and he woulda gone out of business."

He had me now. I'd have to go a couple of rounds to hear the end of his thoughts. We walked up the stairs.

"So you don't think he was a commie."

"I doubt it. Tell ya what. After a coupla rounds, we'll talk about it some more."

'We did a bit of skipping, hit the big bag a bit, then climbed into the ring. After four rounds, it was about even, but I was ready to quit. Or else throw up.

"Ya gettin' soft, Duggan. No stamina. Too much beer."

"Yeah. A couple would go pretty good right about now."

We showered and dressed. I wished I had saved my spare shirt.

We walked over to the Belle Clair, where the sporting crowd hung out.

They had a good veal cutlet plate at the Belle Clair. We ordered a couple, to go along with the draft.

"See, Duggan, from what I know, this Gouzenko guy got all excited at the money over here, and all the food and clothes and stuff he couldn't get back in Russia. So when they wanted to send him back home, he hadda find a ticket to stay over here. So he gathered up all the files he could lay his hands on and took a walk.

"After the *Journal* booted him out on his ass, he went over to the Mounties. They took care of him.

"Every one he named was tossed in jail. He was scared that the Russian secret police, whatever they call them – the KNVD or something – was goin' to nail him, so the Mounties hadda guard him full time. Give him a new identification and all. Far as I know, they still are. One of the Mounties I know told me he's a real pain in the ass."

"Yeah, it makes sense. Carson said that Robinson checked out clean on the commie angle."

"If I were you, I'd look into his personal life more. Probably some reason there. Maybe his wife was foolin' around, and it got to him."

"Yeah."

"What the hell, find a good reason for a suicide real quick and just close it out. Better yet, let the Mounties have it."

"I'd do that in a minute if I was sure they were going to handle it straight. One thing I can't stand is those red-coated buggers comin' into my town and pullin' a fast one on me."

"I know what ya mean. Still, they aren't all bad. That buddy of mine, he's a swell guy. And he was a good cop, too."

"He quit?"

"Retired."

"Say, Bruno, you wouldn't have his number still, would you?"

"You wanna talk to him?"

"Maybe I could check out this Gouzenko lad, see if he ever heard of Robinson."

"Well, I can give you his number. Lives out in the Valley, retired to Renfrew. But I don't think it'll do you any good. Far's I know, they got this Gouzenko good and hid, with his new identity and all. They won't give you anything, I don't think."

"Well, maybe I could just chat up your friend. Never know what might come out of it."

Bruno laughed. "Ya know who could help you out, eh?"

"Who?"

"That Sergeant Carson."

"Thanks a lot, Bruno. Thanks a lot."

Bruno promised me the phone number the next day. We walked back to the station.

I looked over the files I had neglected earlier. There were two coroner's reports. In twenty-three years on the Ottawa force, this was the first time I'd ever had two coroner's reports on my desk at the same time. The one on the girl in the park was to the point. She had been hit once with a heavy, blunt instrument. Maybe a tire iron.

There was one surprising thing. The girl's dental work was not consistent with Canadian standards, and was probably done in Europe. The coroner had written in the margin, "What made you ask, Duggan?" She had had no major operations. She wasn't a virgin, but she hadn't borne a child. She had no rings or jewelry. Other than that, she was the picture of health. Except she was dead.

The report on Robinson was consistent with a fall from seven storeys. It was impossible to tell whether he had been slugged before falling. Other than that, the report was full of grisly detail about breaks, fractures and ruptures. I was depressed.

A dead diplomat who had just returned from Australia and a dead girl who had had dental work done in Europe. Any possible connection seemed far-fetched.

I called Mrs. Robinson. No reply.

Stephen Duckworth was the A.D.M. of External Affairs who had called me earlier. Hitching a ride in a spare squad car, I made my way to his Alta Vista home. It was just past the dinner hour, so I figured he'd probably be there.

Alta Vista was a nice, middle-class area in Ottawa's east end where middle- to upper-level civil servants liked to live. A house in Alta Vista and a cottage in Constance Bay meant you had arrived in Ottawa.

Duckworth lived in a large white split-level, with about an acre of lawn on a corner lot. Everything was neat and tidy. It was a long way from Lowertown.

The house was all lit up like the First of July, and there were about twenty cars parked outside. It looked like Duckworth was having a party. Some fun.

I asked the patrolman to wait a half-hour for me, and if I wasn't out yet to come and get me. He thought he could cruise around, see if he could give out a few traffic tickets. He had the right idea.

A teenage daughter, helping out at Mommy and Daddy's party, answered the door. I asked for Mr. Duckworth. The kid told me to go right into the party. I went in.

Everyone was dressed to the nines except me. I still had on my rumpled shirt.

Someone, probably Mrs. Duckworth, looked at me with what seemed like panic. She went over and whispered something to a tall man with a military bearing. Mr. Duckworth.

Duckworth came charging over. "May I help you?"

I pulled my wallet from my hip pocket. "Detective Duggan, Ottawa Police. You called me earlier today." The partygoers were giving me the once-over. They obviously didn't like what they saw.

"Well, Inspector, this is obviously a bad time. Perhaps sometime tomorrow..."

I was getting a bit fed up, even though he had promoted me. "Look, Mr. Duckworth, I've got two dead bodies on my hands. I don't have a lot of time. Maybe we can find a corner to talk."

He left me abruptly, spoke to his wife, swallowed the rest of what I took to be a glass of good scotch, and led me into a sort of den. He closed the door.

"I don't appreciate this unwarranted invasion of my privacy." He was obviously used to giving orders. I was used to taking them when I had to. Right now, I didn't have to.

"You called me. Why?"

"You must have guessed it was about this Robinson matter." Putting me on the defensive.

"No. I didn't know what you were calling about." I wasn't giving him anything.

"This situation is awkward. I've got a house full of guests. I can't take a lot of time to talk to you."

"Perhaps you'd feel more comfortable if we talked at the station."

"That sounds suspiciously like a threat."

"I was just trying to fit into your plans."

He glared at me. "Maybe we could start all over."

"Fine with me. You called me earlier today."

"I was calling to discuss the ramifications of the death of

Walter Robinson, so far as they affected External Affairs."
Covering his ass.

"And how does it affect External Affairs?"

"You must realize that much of the work we do is conducted
in an atmosphere of mutual trust and confidence and information is not easily bruited about."

He was telling me in his circuitous way that External wasn't
about to help my investigation. "I am the soul of discretion, Mr.
Duckworth."

I got a smile out of him. "I'm sure you are. I can tell by the way
you barged in here tonight."

"I was trying to get your attention."

"It worked. Internal investigation by the department has
revealed that Mr. Robinson apparently committed suicide
because he was deathly afraid of appearing at the House
Un-American Committee hearings in Washington."

Tell me something I haven't heard before. "Did you know
Robinson?"

"I've known him since he entered the service in 1938. Even
before that. I was posted in London when he was attending
Cambridge. Actually, I was the one who recruited him."

"Tell me about his background."

"Walter came from a well-connected family that lived near
London, Ontario. At one time the family was well off, but most
of the money was lost in '29." Nobody I knew lost any money in
'29, because we didn't have any to lose. "Still, there was enough
for young Walter's education. He graduated from McGill, then
took a year or two off to tour Europe and the Far East. Then he
went to Cambridge. Which is when I met him."

"What was he afraid to tell the committee?"

"If I knew anything about that, I still couldn't tell you."

"Well, tell me this: was Robinson some kind of agent, or
involved in security in any way?"

"Canadian diplomats are not spies." His look dared me to
argue.

"If he was involved in highly secret operations, I can
understand his reluctance to testify, and also everyone else's
willingness to cover up for him."

"All diplomatic missions are secret, to one degree or another."

"Everyone says he didn't have anything to tell the committee, anyway. Is that true?"

"Again, I'm not at liberty to divulge that sort of information."

"What about his state of mind these last three weeks. He must have been over at External a lot. What was being discussed?"

Duckworth thought about that for a long minute, as if trying to decide how much to tell me.

"Worried, of course. Maybe you could call it bewildered. He didn't seem to know what to do. You've got to realize this didn't just come up yesterday. The committee first made their allegations three, four years ago. They couldn't make it stick then, and I doubt if they could now."

"From what I read in the newspapers, McCarthy himself is in trouble."

"Poor Walter should have just stuck it out a bit longer. I think the committee itself will be disbanded soon. Mind you, there's always new committees. Once you're branded a subversive, it follows you forever, it seems like." He sounded bitter.

"Well, it's getting late, and I deserve a good sleep tonight. Tell me this, though: both you and the Mounties are doing a good job convincing me that Robinson wasn't a commie, or even a fellow traveller. If that's so, why did he commit suicide? There's something missing."

"The Mounties? Inspector, I can understand your belligerence if you think the Mounties and External are getting together on some cover-up. But nothing could be further from the truth.

"You see, we don't get along with the Mounties at all. They're crude, they're anti-intellectual, and they see subversives under every bed. And they think we're a bunch of slackers, a department full of communists and homosexuals. We're at each other's throats all the time.

"My only concern is that the department doesn't get any bad press out of this. Our main concern is protecting the prime minister. Don't forget, he's defended Robinson on record and in public."

What he said made sense. I hadn't known about the bad feelings between the Mounties and External.

"You got anything else for me?" He shook his head. Just then, the constable came to the door, causing another stir. Duckworth would have a lot of explaining to do to his guests.

As I walked out the door, Duckworth put his hand on my arm. "Inspector? You mentioned two dead bodies."

Sometimes I talk too much. It comes with the gift of the gab. I shrugged. "Not connected. But it makes for twice the work. We're a small department." He seemed to accept that.

I hitched a ride in the squad car back to the station.

CHAPTER 7

Sometimes the luck of the Irish actually works. Back at the station I was staring at the walls. I was trying to think, but it was too hot, I was tired, and no thoughts came.

Around ten, I got a call from a Constable Turner. I didn't remember any Constable Turner. But it turned out that Turner had been supplied with a picture of the dead woman in the park, and he had done some freelance work showing it around his own neighbourhood after supper.

It had paid off. He had found the apartment where she lived, on Somerset near Bank Street.

I thanked him profusely, and promised all sorts of rewards I would never be able to grant him. He gave me the address.

I wandered up to Burglary, and borrowed the set of burglar's tools we kept on hand for just such occasions. I hung around until there was a spare squad car and then hitched a ride to Somerset and Bank.

It was a plain, six-apartment building, built about forty years earlier, but kept in reasonably good shape.

After standing in the shadows across the street for a half-hour, I walked over. It was just past midnight.

It only took a minute to jimmy the lock on apartment 4-B. I stepped inside the blackness.

Had I been so careless during the war, I'd be dead now.

I sensed movement before I saw anything. I was just reaching into my hip pocket for identification when a dark form came rushing at me and knocked me down.

Nothing I like better than a good brawl. I leapt to my feet, braced myself and waited for his attack. It never came.

Instead, I was hit from behind by a second attacker. I cursed my stupidity as I fell.

The beating was professional and meticulous. Apart from the first smash to my head, they concentrated on my body. I tried to roll into a tight ball, but their fists and boots found my tender parts again and again. I was almost unconscious from the pain. I knew several ribs were cracked or broken, and my kidneys would be tender for a long time. They were both big men, and they had been taught how to hurt somebody. I wished it hadn't been me.

When I was helpless, one of them gave me a final vicious kick, then they both sauntered out, closing the door quietly. Nice touch.

I lay there for fifteen minutes, waiting for the pain to go away. It didn't. Slowly, I got to my feet and turned on a small table lamp.

Every movement was agony. I walked about, clutching my abdomen.

All the curtains were closed, so I flipped on a few more lights. The apartment was a mess. It had been ripped apart once, twice, maybe a third time. Whoever it had been deserved top marks for thoroughness.

I tried looking around, but I could hardly walk for the pain. The telephone still worked, so I called the station for a squad car and two officers.

It looked like whoever had been here had removed anything giving a clue to the identity of the person who lived there. In a garbage bin, one scrap of paper seemed to have the name "Tina" on it, but then it could be part of a longer word.

I sat and waited for the two officers. Leaving one to search the apartment more thoroughly, I asked the other to give me a lift to the General Hospital. It was in my neighbourhood, and I could get home from there. I sent the patrolman back to pick up his partner. I told him to leave a report on my desk for the morning. I didn't expect much from it.

The nurse told me I had a couple of cracked ribs. She cheered me up by explaining that cracked ribs were often more painful than broken ones.

She also told me that I would probably stop passing blood in my urine in a day or two.

Sister Mary Agnes walked by. I tried to hide. No luck.

"Pendrick Duggan! Just three months ago you promised me you'd not be back here for at least a couple of years. What happened now?"

I lied. "Well, sister, it's like this. I was just walking home, and I saw a burglary in progress. I thought there was just the one of them, but there really were two. They resisted arrest."

"Well, at least I hope you stopped the robbery."

"No such luck, Sister."

She helped me to the front door. Sister Mary Agnes and I had gone to school together and I still kidded her about it. "My offer still stands, Sister."

She smiled. "I'll not be leavin' the sisterhood for any man, Duggan. And certainly not for a policeman. And especially not for such a poor specimen as yourself, who can't even stop a robbery in progress."

I liked Sister Mary Agnes, but she did have a sharp tongue.

I walked up to St. Patrick and caught the streetcar home. It would be nice to lie between clean, cool sheets. If I had clean, cool sheets on my bed.

At least there was the left-over beer from last night. A few shots of brandy would go better.

First a cup of tea. Then the beer. Maybe just go straight to bed. I couldn't decide. It was too hot to sleep. I was too sore to stay awake. What's a man to do?

In the event, I sat at the kitchen table, and fell asleep with my head cradled in my arms.

When I awoke four hours later, my sore back fit in with all the rest of my aches and pains.

It was too early to get ready for work, so I decided to sit in the shade of the front porch to watch the sun come up.

I don't normally start drinking until noon, but this was a special occasion, so I opened one and sipped it slowly.

I could hear the sounds of the milkman's horse a couple of

streets over. They were talking of replacing the horses with trucks. Too bad.

I sat and felt sorry for myself. I had to get some sort of order into these investigations. I was just running from one event to the next. Not the way I was taught.

The coolness of the shade felt good. It was going to be another hot day. When would it end?

By the time I was half-way through my second beer, the milkman turned up Papineau. I hid my beer. It wouldn't do for the milkman to see me drinking beer at five in the morning.

I bought a quart of milk and went inside to see about breakfast.

I put the water on to boil for tea, then put some butter into the frying pan for the eggs. I bought my eggs from Mrs. Prevost next door. Like lots of my neighbours, the Prevosts kept chickens in their back yard, and made a few extra pennies selling eggs. They were talking of outlawing the keeping of chickens within the city limits. The poor get poorer.

When I had cracked two eggs into the pan, I popped open the milk and, using a spoon, licked up all the rich cream which lay at the top.

They don't sell real milk any more. They have this stuff they call milk, but it isn't the same. It doesn't look the same, doesn't taste the same. Milk should be yellow, not white. And it should have cream sitting on top.

Come to think of it, eggs don't taste like eggs any more, either. People can't keep chickens in their back yard.

We don't even want to discuss the stuff they call butter today. What kind of society would give up the taste of real food?

I sliced up a couple of pieces of bread to toast on the stove. That's another thing. Today, only foreigners make real bread. I have a rule of thumb: if it's already sliced, it's not real bread.

I turned on the radio for the six a.m. news. Emilie Dionne, one of the Dionne quints, had died at age twenty. She had had an epileptic seizure while visiting a convent. Too bad. A couple of guys had run a mile in less than four minutes in Vancouver. In Germany, bunches of spies were defecting to East Germany one step ahead of the authorities. I wished Robinson had defected instead of dying on one of my streets.

After two cups of tea, I felt better. It was time to go see Sergeant Carson.

I bathed, dressed and shaved. It was getting hotter.

I got off the streetcar in front of the justice building on Wellington Street, where the Mounties had their headquarters.

I showed my identification to a bored-looking constable, and asked for Carson. I heard him ask for Special Branch on the telephone. Special Branch? I wondered what Special Branch did, but knew I'd probably not like the answer.

Presently, Carson came down. It was the first time I had seen him in uniform. He looked good.

"Duggan! Good to see you. Come on in. Coffee? Tea?" He was being pretty friendly. We went into what looked like an interrogation room. He poured a coffee and a tea. "So. What's new?"

"Where is she, Carson?"

"Where is who, Duggan?"

"The grieving widow."

"Ah, you mean Mrs. Robinson."

"I mean Mrs. Robinson, yes."

It appeared he was going to lie, but changed his mind at the last second. "I understand she's visiting friends."

"You might well understand, since you took her there."

"What does it matter? You're off this case anyway."

"Not till two o'clock this afternoon."

"That's only a few hours away."

I put on what I hoped was an aggrieved look. "Maybe I'll skip the meeting."

Carson put on what he hoped was a bored look. "It wouldn't really matter. That so-called file of yours is so thin it probably wouldn't help us, anyway." He didn't know how right he was. Then he stood up and stared intently into my eyes. I continued sipping my tea.

"Anyway, Duggan. You've been holding out on me."

"How so?"

"Katrina Voscovitch. Thought we didn't know about that, didn't you?"

Now I had a name for the dead girl. I had somehow got a bit

fond of thinking of her as The Girl In The Park. "I was just going to tell you. Anyway, what's a dead girl to you?" I already knew the answer.

"Any foreign national found dead in this country becomes the concern of the RCM Police."

He had just given me a truckload of information I hadn't known. Had he done it on purpose, or did he think I already knew these things?

"How's the ribs, Duggan?" He knew. I had a sudden thought that the two goons could be Mounties. It made me angry.

"You arrange that, Carson? If so..."

He turned pale, and came around to my side of the table. "Of course not. We don't operate like that." He smiled reassuringly. "Besides, you're useful to us, with that bull in the china shop routine. You stir things up, and we pick up the pieces."

I wasn't sure if he was telling the truth or not. When I said nothing, something seem to dawn on him. "You do know who Katrina Voscovitch is, don't you, Duggan?"

I took a stab in the dark. "Yeah. She's a Russian cipher clerk." I sipped at my tea, not meeting his eyes.

"Well, something like that. Officially she's a translator. But really she's an NKVD operative. I think now they're starting to call the NKVD the KGB."

It was all a mess of meaningless initials to me. "Sort of the Russian RCMP."

He laughed. "More like the Gestapo than the Mounties."

"So. Did we kill her or did they?"

"If you mean the mounties by 'we', it sure wasn't us. But you've been investigating that one, not me."

"I found out her name, occupation and address. Not much else."

"Did you get a look at the guys who pounded you out?"

Now, that was the funny thing. It was pitch dark in that apartment, but I could swear that I would recognize one of the men if I saw him again, just from the way he stood, the way he held his head, the shape of his nose, the feel of the cloth of his suit. I didn't tell Carson that. "Not really. It was too dark."

"Did you find anything of interest in the apartment?"

"I don't know, yet. I left two officers behind to search, and I haven't read their report yet."

"I understand the apartment had already been searched."

"Say, Carson, how is it that you know all this stuff?"

Carson smiled. He was enjoying my mystification. "Just say a little birdie told me. You may think this is your town, Duggan, but we have our sources, too."

Enough sparring. "I'm sure you have a lot of work to do, Carson, so if you give me a number where I can reach Mrs. Robinson, I'll be on my way."

"And if I refuse?"

I thought about that for awhile, as I put my hat on. "If she's in town, I'll find her, Carson. It might take awhile, but I'll find her. It only took me one day to find out where that Katrina person lived."

"I was impressed by that, Duggan. Probably just dumb luck." He didn't know how right he was.

"Francis said this investigation was to give me information and involvement. You're stalling on your part already."

"The deal doesn't begin until two o'clock."

I turned to leave. "The deal is off, as of right now."

"CEntral 5-5221."

"Thanks, Carson. Pleasure dealing with you."

He yelled at me as I strode out the door, "Don't forget. You find anything in that apartment I should know, you tell me."

"Sure thing, Carson."

The last thing I heard as I walked out the front door was Carson's laughter.

I grabbed a streetcar to the corner of Rideau and Nicholas, and walked over to the station.

As I expected, nothing of interest had been found in the apartment. I did have the pleasure of replacing 'Last Name Unknown, First Name Unknown' with 'Voscovitch, Katrina' on the file.

Bruno came by with the phone number of the Mountie who had spent some time with Igor Gouzenko. I called him, and made an appointment to meet him later that morning. His name was Ed Lukowicz. I didn't tell him what I wanted to talk to him about. Maybe he wouldn't have invited me over.

Renfrew was about an hour's drive outside Ottawa. I called my brother, Ken. Maybe he could give me a lift out.

Ken had started a small construction firm after the war, which was still struggling to get off the ground nine years later. He lived in Eastview. Housing was cheap in Eastview. Even cheaper than Lowertown.

"Doing anything this morning, Ken?"

"Not a hell of a lot."

"How would you like to take a drive in the country?"

"You paying for the gas?"

I offered to pay for the gas, hoping the Chief would authorize reimbursement later, and Ken agreed to drive his truck over to the station in a half-hour.

I knew better than to ask Ken how business was. For some reason, other contractors were doing better than him, even though his work was of a high quality, and his prices were reasonable. I always thought it was his lack of personality when dealing with the public. His trouble was that his firm was too small. If he had a bigger company, he could afford to hire a professional salesman. And if he had a salesman on staff, his business would grow.

We talked about the weather. We talked about his wife, Rita, and his two kids, Charles and Daniel. We talked about the upcoming Rocky Marciano–Ezzard Charles fight. I bet five dollars on Charles. We didn't talk about police work or the construction business.

We found Lukowicz's house without much trouble. He had a huge front lawn, and was sitting at a picnic table under a huge tree with a pitcher of something cold in front of him.

Ken waited by the truck.

I sat down after shaking hands, placing my hat, jacket and tie on the table.

Lukowicz wasn't as big as I expected for a Mountie, he looked slightly shrunken, by age or tribulation. Maybe retirement does that to you. Maybe I'm smaller now than I used to be.

He had a habit of darting his eyes everywhere while he spoke, as if he expected enemies to come charging across his lawn. He poured us each a glass of lemonade, which tasted like it was liberally spiked with gin. I smiled.

"That's a good drink, Mr. Lukowicz."

"Thanks. My wife objects to my drinking, so I have to disguise it any way I can." His eyes darted nervously about. "What can I do for you, Detective?"

I told him the story of the dead diplomat. Maybe I implied a little more cooperation between the Mounties and me than was the case.

"I hope that maybe you can give me a little off-the-record information about how this might possibly fit in with the Gouzenko case a few years back. I understand you were in on that one."

"Gouzenko? How would he fit into this?" I explained Bruno's theory about Gouzenko turning in all the Canadian spies working for the Russians.

He got up. "I was assigned to protect Gouzenko for about a year. This was a few years after he defected. Tell you the truth, I never did like the man. He was a real pain in the ass." He stood, watching the highway carefully. "Maybe I'm wrong, but I don't like defectors, no matter which side they're on. I wouldn't like a Canadian who ratted on his country, and I don't like a Russian who does it."

He poured two new glasses of lemonade. He wondered if my brother would like some. I said he wouldn't. He had to drive us back to Ottawa.

"I know what you're trying to do here, Detective. Trying to close down one avenue of investigation, so's you can concentrate on another. It's a nice try, but it's not going to work."

I wondered why not.

"You see, a lot of the stuff Gouzenko brought over was still in the form of codes. He could break a lot of it, but there were still people's code names that we never did find out.

"I hate to admit it, but we screwed up a lot. It's understandable, it was this country's first big spy case. We prosecuted a lot of people on the wrong charges and they got off. But, worse than that, we never did crack open all the code names.

"You see, after awhile, the whole thing became sort of an embarrassment. My opinion is the government wasn't really interested in finding any more spies.

"For awhile, there was a conscientious officer who kept working for months, maybe years, trying to make head or tails out of the files. There were a lot of them. But he was discouraged by his superiors, and the box of papers went back into the basement."

He was right, I had tried to close down at least one area of investigation. It wasn't working out.

"And, to make things worse, I've got more bad news for you. A couple of months ago, the government let Gouzenko talk to some American national security committee again. Now, the official word is that he didn't tell them anything new. That's the official word.

"What you'd like to know is if maybe Gouzenko told them something about this Robinson fellow."

I was getting depressed. I thanked him for his cooperation. I wondered if it might be possible to locate and talk to this Gouzenko fellow. He thought that would be impossible.

"Thanks for the visit, Detective. I enjoyed talking with you. Drop out again sometime."

I promised I would.

"One last thing. I think I know someone who might be able to give you more up-to-date information."

"That's very nice of you. Who would that be?"

"There's a fellow in headquarters you should talk to. Sergeant name of Carson."

"Thanks a lot, Mr. Lukowicz."

The drive back to Ottawa was silent. As we approached the outskirts of Ottawa, it occurred to me that everyone was right: I should make my peace with the Mounties. Perhaps Carson and I wouldn't make such a bad team.

Immediately I decided that, I felt better. Ken and I discussed the possibilities of a winning season for the Ottawa Athletics of the International Baseball League. Unfortunately, Ottawa was twenty-seven games out of first place. Neither one of us held out much hope.

I told Ken the story of the Athletics' leading hitter, Joe Taylor. It seems that Joe had been arrested for impaired driving in Hull. When he was convicted, he announced he'd spend the seven days in jail, rather than pay the hundred-dollar fine.

Someone from the ball club came by in the afternoon and paid his fine. He was needed on the field.

"At least he got a free lunch in jail."

"Well, maybe not a free one. A hundred-dollar lunch."

"Free for Joe, though."

CHAPTER 8

I was only a few minutes late for my meeting with the Chief and Superintendent Francis. This second meeting went much better than the first. I had beefed up the file on Robinson so that it looked reasonable. The only things I hadn't mentioned were the meeting with Lukowicz and the murder of Katrina Voscovitch. We were all getting along so well, the Chief was even smiling. I ended the meeting by remarking that it was possible Robinson had committed suicide, but I still wasn't sure.

He thanked me and left.

Still full of the spirit of cooperation, I phoned Carson. I was kept waiting for a full five minutes before he came on the line.

"Duggan, how are you? How'd the meeting go with Francis?"

"All is roses."

"Good news. We'll get to the bottom of this in no time at all."

"In the spirit of all this cooperation, I thought I'd consult you about this second case, the death of Katrina Voscovitch."

"Yeah? What can I do for you?" He was being remarkably cheerful and helpful.

"Well, I suppose somebody has got to notify the embassy. I don't suppose she's got any relatives over here. Is that my job or yours?"

"Tell you what, Duggan. You go in first, and I'll come in when somebody comes to identify the body." That sounded good to me.

Since it was official police business, I was able to commandeer a squad car and driver. I got the driver to stop by my place so I could change into some clean, dry clothes.

We pulled up across the street from the embassy. It looked cold and foreboding, like I imagined all buildings in the socialist paradise to be. I straightened my hat and walked up to the front door.

A small peep-door opened to my knock. I showed my identification, asked to see the ambassador, and was told to wait.

After ten minutes or so, the peep-door opened once more and I was told it was impossible to see the ambassador. I should phone for an appointment. The door closed.

I knocked again. I admitted I would see someone else. Perhaps the assistant ambassador. I still couldn't see the person I was talking to. As the door was closing once more on my face, I shouted, "It's a matter of life and death." That didn't seem to impress whoever was behind the door.

I waited another ten minutes. I guess they saw I wasn't going away, for finally the door was opened. A thin young man with prematurely balding, straw-blond hair stood aside to let me in. He wasn't smiling, so I smiled broadly and stuck out my hand. He didn't take it. Probably thought I was a capitalist running dog or something.

He led me into a small reception room just inside the doorway. There was a picture of Joe Stalin on the wall. It occurred to me that Joe Stalin was dead. I couldn't remember who had replaced him. I sat on the one settee. In front of me was a clean desk and a chair.

Presently, two men came in. The shorter, younger and stouter man did the talking.

"I am Nikola Cherniak, translator. This is Illych Krupotkin, third secretary. Identification, please."

I produced my wallet. Nikola phoned the police station to ascertain I was who I said I was. He explained to Illych that I seemed genuine. "How may we help you, Mr. Duggan?"

I consulted my empty notebook. "You have an employee here by the name of Katrina Voscovitch?"

They huddled together. Nikola admitted they had such a person on staff.

"She has not been into work lately." I glared at them. They glared back.

Illych said something in Russian to Nikola. Nikola rattled something back. They glared at me again. Finally, Nikola spoke.

"The third secretary believes it is of no concern to the police whether one of our employees is at work or not."

I persisted. "Do you know where Miss Voscovitch is right this minute?"

They chatted between themselves. Illych started for the door. Nikola translated. "The third secretary says that you have no jurisdiction here. Please to leave. Miss Voscovitch is travelling on embassy business. I shall escort you to the door."

"She's dead."

Illych stopped dead in his tracks, his hand on the doorknob. He knew some English, that was certain.

"At least we believe the dead woman is Katrina Voscovitch." I made a show of consulting my notebook. Nikola made a show of translating for Illych, who then returned to the desk, barking sharply.

"The third secretary is convinced you're mistaken."

"What I would like is for someone who knows Miss Voscovitch to accompany me to the police station. If we are mistaken, I offer my sincerest apologies." I had the sudden thought that I had only Carson's word that the dead lady in the park was this Katrina. I hadn't thought to ask him how he was so certain. Of course, had I done that, I would have revealed my own ignorance. It's seldom you'll find Pendrick Duggan doing that.

They both agreed to follow me to the station. I asked for a phone. I called Carson and asked him to meet us there in fifteen minutes. He agreed. I held back a smile at the thought that, if the Mounties were bugging the embassy phones, some Mountie somewhere would now be a bit perplexed.

The four of us stared down at the naked body. Suddenly, Illych started screaming, waving his arms and turning red in the face. He pointed his finger accusingly at me.

When he calmed down, Nikola turned to me. "The third secretary would like to know if this is your idea of a joke?"

"What are you talking about?"

"We have never seen this woman before."

"Are you trying to tell me this is not Katrina Voscovitch?"

Illych started up again. Nikola translated. "The third secretary wishes you to know that the Soviet Union will send a stiff note of protest to your government, demanding an immediate, full and abject apology. We have no idea who this woman is, but she is not an embassy employee."

I gulped and turned to Carson, a sinking feeling in my stomach. What the hell?

Carson was smooth, I'll give him that. He folded his arms calmly across his chest.

"You deny that this is Katrina Voscovitch, who lives at 342 Somerset Street?"

They chatted again. "We deny nothing. However, we do state that this is not Katrina Voscovitch."

"Back at the embassy, they maintained Miss Voscovitch was travelling," I helpfully informed Carson.

"If that's so, she will be within a hundred and fifty miles. Would you please give us a phone number or an address where she can be reached."

They consulted in Russian. All this translation business was getting on my nerves. There was no way I could ever work at the United Nations.

"We shall do no such thing. We shall leave. Your Department of External Affairs will hear about this."

Carson and I walked them outside. A uniformed chauffeur opened the rear door for them.

I had a sudden headache.

I knew that chauffeur. The last time I had glimpsed him, he was putting the boots to my poor, aching body.

The car drove away. I had the feeling I had been set up. I turned to Carson, my fists clenched.

Carson smiled. "Buy you a beer, Duggan?"

I didn't smile. "During working hours?"

"Doesn't seem to be against the rules around here."

"For all the explaining you're going to have to do, Carson, it'll be more than one beer."

We found a table at the Albion. Carson had a big grin on his face. I had a scowl on mine.

"What's this hundred and fifty miles business?"

"Russians aren't allowed to travel more than that far from Ottawa."

"Oh." There were a lot of things I didn't know about this diplomatic business.

"Why tell me the girl was this Voscovitch?"

"I thought you had already come up with that name."

"I never heard it before you mentioned it."

"I thought so. Well, they played it that way, and we'll have to see where they take it. Probably just stalling for time."

"You mean it really is Voscovitch?"

"As far as I know."

I was sorely confused. I gulped down the two drafts, ordered two more. I didn't offer to pay. After a moment, Carson reluctantly took out his wallet.

"Is she or isn't she? No bullshit."

"Either she is Voscovitch, or they're running someone else under that name. Either way, they're going to have trouble explaining all the confusion."

"Why would they deny it?"

"Think, Duggan, think. It would seem to me that they don't know who killed her. And they want to know the answer to that before they admit anything."

"What's it got to do with Robinson?"

"Nothing, as far as I know. What makes you ask that?"

I had forgotten that I was the only one who knew about the phone call. "Nothing, really. I was just following the logic of Robinson's commie connections and a dead Russian. Nothing there, eh?"

"Nothing, and you can trust me on that one." I knew he was lying, and I didn't trust him.

"Well, now you've got the Robinson case from me. I suppose you'll want this one, too."

"Duggan, we're all police officers. It's not a matter of taking cases away, it's a matter of solving them together."

"I believe the Russians. She's not this Katrina."

"What on earth makes you say that?"

"Don't know. Just a feeling."

"Our identification is pretty solid."

"Tell you what, Carson. I stopped trying to find out the girl's identity because I thought you had given it to me. Now I'm going to verify it for myself. That's what I should have done in the first place."

"You'll be wasting valuable police time, Duggan. And you'll find out she's Voscovitch."

"Maybe. But at least I'll be certain. See you, Carson." I left him. He was still on his first draft.

It was still hot, but I didn't notice it as much today. Maybe I was getting used to it.

Back at the station, in an effort to become more methodical, I made a list of all the things I should be doing.

First, I should talk to the guy who found the girl in the park (I had gone back to my original name for her, Voscovitch now being in question).

Second, I should talk to Mrs. Robinson again.

Third, I should find out who had rented that apartment on Somerset Street.

I should also check with Carson about that new information the Senator had mentioned.

I figured checking out the apartment would take the most time, so I left it until the morning.

If I completed the other three tasks today, I thought, I might treat myself to a movie. I flipped through a newspaper, checking the listings. Joel McCrea was playing in *Black Horse Canyon* at the Centre. There was a new Lewis and Martin comedy, *Scared Stiff*, at the Century. The best bet seemed to be *She Couldn't Say No*, with Robert Mitchum and Jean Simmons at the Regent. I liked Robert Mitchum. Jean Simmons wasn't hard to take, either.

I called the guy who had found the girl in the park.

His name was Luc Gerrard. I had forgotten he was a civil servant. He was long gone from the office. So much for my movie. I was always serious about these little deals I made with myself.

I called CEntral 5-5221, identified myself and asked for Mrs. Robinson. She came on the line immediately.

"Mr. Duggan? How nice to hear from you. Sergeant Carson said that you probably would never be in touch with me again." Carson would.

"Just a few things I forgot to ask you, Mrs. Robinson. Is it possible that we could meet later tonight?"

She thought it was possible. We debated about several possible meeting places and finally decided on her room at the Chateau Laurier. Seven o'clock.

"You do know that Walter's funeral is tomorrow morning?" I didn't. Time had moved so fast, I hadn't realized he had died two days ago. I promised to be there.

I called Constable Turner, and made arrangements to meet him at his place at eight the next morning. Together, we'd check out the apartment on Somerset.

Bruno came by to chat. I brought him up to date and thanked him for putting me in touch with Lukowicz.

"Say, Duggan, I'm not doing anything tomorrow morning. How's about I tag along with you?" I suggested that we all could meet at Turner's at eight. He had a better idea, breakfast at the Party Palace on Elgin at seven. We agreed.

I sat thinking about the Russian chauffeur for awhile. I wanted to chat him up a little, but wasn't sure how to go about it.

I'd figure something out.

As I walked through the Chateau's lobby, a bellman gestured me over. He was a fat, balding fifty. He sweated a lot and talked with a mild French accent.

"Monsieur, is it possible to inquire who the fat gentleman is that you were talking to in this lobby two days ago?" It seemed funny, him calling another man fat.

I admitted it was possible, but asked why he wanted to know.

He asked if I was investigating the suicide of the gentleman who had jumped out the window. I admitted that was also possible.

Then, the clincher. If he had some pertinent information, was it possible that he would be paid for this information?

I disabused him of that notion fast and told him to start talking.

He was very hurt. However, he said that he had seen the fat gentleman visiting Mr. Robinson several times in the week before he died, sometimes accompanied by as many as five other men.

"When was the last time you saw him go up?"

He got my attention. "The night before the gentleman died."

"Did you see him leave?"

He admitted he hadn't, but that it was still possible the Senator had left unnoticed by him.

It was interesting. I didn't know what it meant, but it was interesting.

Mrs. Robinson had on a different black dress. It looked every bit as good as the first one.

She offered me scotch, brandy or Canadian Club. No tea this time. I took the Canadian Club, two ice cubes, no water. She took a snifter of brandy. For her health.

"Have your investigations been fruitful, Mr. Duggan?" I admitted that I had had more fruitful investigations. Then, I took the picture of the girl in the park out of my pocket and showed it to her.

"Have you ever seen this woman before?"

She looked at it for a long moment, then shook her head. "Who is she?"

"I don't know yet. You're sure you never saw her in the company of your husband?"

"I'm sure." She walked around the suite, rearranging things. "Why do you think she knew my husband? And what difference would it make?"

I lied shamelessly. "I was just looking for a personal angle to your husband's suicide. I'm not sure which answer would hurt you the least, but I like to know the truth about things, no matter what I write in the official report."

She looked interested that I might write an official report which was different from the truth.

"Do you do that often, Mr. Duggan?"

"On occasion. When the truth hurts people, and it doesn't matter anyway."

"I'm positive I've never seen that woman before. And definitely not in the company of my husband."

Another dead end. Well, I keep trying.

"Carson seems to think that a bunch of your husband's old Cambridge friends were commies, and that he should have reported them to the Americans during the war. What do you think of that story?"

She poured us each another one. "Not much."

I sipped my drink, watching her, expecting her to say something more. She didn't.

I walked over to the window and opened it. The sound of traffic and the warm evening air came in.

"Let's see. He came over to the window, he stood up on this ledge, he opened the window, then..."

"Stop, stop!" She ran over to the door. "Can't you do that when you're all alone?"

I climbed down from the ledge. "I didn't mean to upset you."

"Well, you did a fine job of it!"

Idly, I picked up a pawn from the chess board. "Do you play chess, Mrs. Robinson?"

"No...that is, I used to play chess with Walter when we were first married, but he got so good at it, it wasn't any fun anymore." She took the pawn from me and placed it gently on the set.

"Did you know Walter was an expert chess player, Mr. Duggan? He even wrote two books about chess."

"No, I didn't know that."

She walked into the bedroom, beckoning me to follow her. From a stack of books on the bedside table, she extracted two. I looked them over. *Advanced Chess Strategy*, by W.L. Robinson, and *From Opening Move to End-Game*, also by W.L. Robinson. I was impressed.

Mrs. Robinson sat on the bed. I looked down at her. "Mrs. Robinson, I want to tell you something. I know you're holding back some information from me." She looked up into my eyes. It was not a seductive look, nor was it plaintive. But my whole being felt sad, for her, for this moment, for everything.

"But I'm not," she said, quietly and with conviction.

"I know you're not telling me everything you know, and I know Carson and the Mounties are helping you cover up.

"But let me tell you this: in a few weeks, or a few months, the Mounties will forget all about you, they'll be onto other, more important things. But I won't. I'll keep going, keep digging, until I know the truth."

She stood up, smoothed her dress and, with great dignity, moved once more into the living room. I followed her.

"What is it you think I know, Mr. Duggan?"

"Your husband had visitors the night before he died. Who was it?"

"Visitors? Why don't you tell me who they were?"

"I'd rather you told me."

She sat on the chesterfield. Tears slowly rolled down her cheeks.

"You never let up, do you, Mr. Duggan?" She wiped the tears away. "You may be right, you know, but I wouldn't know. All right, I haven't told you everything. And you know why? For the silliest reason of all. I wanted you to like me."

I stared at her. I didn't know what to say.

"Isn't that silly? I haven't told you the truth because I wanted you to like me."

She wiped her tears away, sat up straight.

"All right, I'll tell you the truth. Walter and I were out that night all right, but we went out separately.

"When I got home around eleven, Walter was already here. I was a little tipsy, so I went straight into bed. Okay, the truth: I was bombed, loaded, pie-eyed. When I hit the bed, I passed out immediately. And don't ask me where I was, or who I was with, because I won't tell you.

"The truth is, Walter could have had a dozen visitors before eleven and I wouldn't have known because I wasn't here. And he could have had a dozen after eleven and I wouldn't have heard, because I was passed out."

I finished my drink and poured myself another one. I couldn't say I was surprised.

"Could Walter have been depressed enough about the state of your marriage that it caused him to commit suicide?"

She finished her own drink and poured another. "Don't you think I've asked myself that question a million times?"

I thought about all the different ways his note could be interpreted. The 'explanations' that were too late could be Mrs. Robinson's, rather than his.

"But I don't think so, Mr. Duggan."

"I don't either, Mrs. Robinson."

I requisitioned a pistol out of stores.

"Goin' huntin', Duggan?" asked Sergeant Sauvier.

"Feel more like the fox than the hound, Sauvier."

Sauvier hadn't gone overseas in the war and, with the shortage of policemen, had been quickly promoted to Sergeant. Later, his lack of overseas service had always counted against him and he was never promoted again. It made him sharp and bitter.

I had no idea whether a chauffeur stayed overnight in an embassy, or whether he went home, but I thought I'd spend a few hours hanging about near the Russian embassy to see if I could get a line on one particular chauffeur.

The ground floor was dark but there were lights gleaming from the third and fourth floors. I counted four people entering and seven leaving in the first two hours. An evening breeze made it a little easier to stand quiet in the nook I had found myself across the street from the embassy.

During the war, I learned how to stand silent and still in the black night for hours at a stretch, never giving eye contact to passersby, becoming an unmoving shadow against a dark building or in an invisible nook. For some reason of timing, I had a reputation in the police force for being incredibly lucky on a stakeout, for while other officers spent weeks waiting for a break, it seemed that when Duggan came along, the quarry always showed itself. Tonight, as always, my luck held.

His bulk and his walk made him easy to spot, since I had seen him twice. I eased myself from the shadows as he turned onto Laurier Avenue.

I played it trickier than I had to, played it tricky like I remembered from the war.

He didn't hear or see me. I put the gun behind his ear and jabbed it. He stood very still. "Let's take a walk, Ivan." He started to raise his arms. "Keep your hands down by your side."

"My name is not Ivan. You have made a mistake."

"Start walking, Ivan."

I walked him to the station and into an interrogation room. I handcuffed his hands behind his back and pushed him into a chair.

"So. Your name is not Ivan. What is it?"

"I wish a telephone. I am entitled to one phone call."

"You've been watching too many American movies, Ivan. You're in Canada now, and up here, you're not entitled to anything. No phone call. No lawyer. Not until you're charged with something."

"I wish to invoke diplomatic immunity. I am a registered employee of the Union of Soviet Socialist Republics." It sounded like he had memorized that line, in case it came in handy some day.

I was getting a little hot under the collar. I locked the door. Then, picking him up by the hair, I slammed him head-first into the wall. He fell awkwardly. Taking up his hair, I did it a second time. Then a third. Blood started pouring down his forehead.

I knew the hot feeling of excitement I felt was sinful. Too late now. I'd go to confession later.

I slammed him into the chair once more.

"What you're entitled to, Ivan, is to play a little game with me. The object of this game is that I ask you some questions, and you answer them. If you don't answer, or if you give the wrong answer, you forfeit. And, if you forfeit, you pay the penalty. And the penalty is another little game to see which will crack first, your head or that wall over there."

The game began. I asked the questions. He didn't answer. He ran head-first into the wall.

It took about a half-dozen questions before I realized that it wasn't going to work. He wasn't saying anything. If I had more privacy and more time, I could make him talk. I had seen it done before. If you have enough privacy and enough time, you can make a man eager, even grateful, to give you all the information you are looking for. You can make him cry with gratitude for a single kind word.

I didn't have the place or the time. So I just copied out all the information in his wallet, towelled off his blood and took him outside. I pushed him a block up Waller Street, took off the handcuffs and threw him into some bushes. I left him there.

Childish, Duggan, childish. My ribs hurt. But I felt a lot better about getting some of my own back. Go to bed, Duggan, go to bed. It's been a long day.

I made a cold roast beef sandwich and put on a pot of tea. I was tired. I took my tea and sandwich to the living room and looked through my collection of records. I had a new set of Billie Holiday records I wanted to hear.

I sank into the easy chair as she sang "All of Me". That took me back to the wartime. Lester Young on tenor saxophone and Eddie Heywood on piano. I could sink into oblivion when Billie sang.

When I was younger, my mother used to get mad when I listened to music like this. She called it 'Jiggerband music'. She hated it. I never knew what the word meant, but I finally figured out it must be a combination of 'jitterbug' and 'nigger'.

We were never allowed to use that word in conversation. I recall, when I was about six or seven years old, my mother and I were on the bus and I pointed to a little boy across the aisle and said, "Look at that little nigger boy." My mother smacked me a good one across the head. She had a strong right arm and was not adverse to using it as a weapon of discipline. When I stopped crying and asked, "What's wrong?", she merely said, "Don't ever say that word again." I automatically knew what word she was referring to, and to this day I've never said it out loud. I've used frog and limey and wop and kike and jap, but I've never used that word.

It's funny about that being the only forbidden word. As I recall, what I was taught when I was a kid was that there were only two nationalities worth considering, Irish and Canadian. Everyone else was inferior in some way. The Brits were lowest on the totem pole because they had caused the most troubles for Ireland and because they came to Canada and took all the good jobs. All Americans were arrogant racists. Also, they never came into a war until there was money to be made and they were sure which was the winning side. Having spent six years in Europe during the last war, I knew that part was true at least. The French were beneath consideration as a civilized people. For some reason, Spaniards were okay. All coloured people were beyond the pale. I'm not saying I still believe all this stuff. It's just the way I was brought up.

I didn't care. I still loved Billie Holiday. She was singing "Mean To Me" now. Lester Young on tenor sax again, Teddy Wilson on piano, Cozy Cole on drums. If I weren't a policeman, I'd like to be a jazz musician. If I knew the first thing about playing a musical instrument. The Irish put a lot of faith in music. But they put even more faith in violence. And they put more faith in booze than they do in violence. Canadians don't put a lot of faith in anything.

I fell asleep thinking once more that I had to put more discipline and order into the investigation. I was acting like an American cop, trusting too much to intuition and luck, and not enough on logic and procedure.

I don't always follow my own advice.

CHAPTER 9

I was up at six. I didn't want to dream any more. A gentle bath. Still passing blood.

I took out my dark blue funeral suit. Shrugged carefully into a clean white shirt. Time to do a laundry soon. I was knotting my tie in front of the hall mirror when I saw the two men on the front porch. I opened it just as one was reaching to knock. They were dressed identically in black shoes, dark suits, white shirts, dark ties. No hats.

One looked to be about fifty, with grey hair carefully combed to hide a bald spot. He was well over six feet and would have weighed in at about two hundred and fifty if he was in the ring, which is where he probably spent a lot of time twenty-five years ago. His nose had undergone a realignment once or twice and he had scar tissue over both of his eyes. There wasn't a single thing about him that was unprofessional.

The other weighed in about seventy pounds less and stood an inch or two shorter. He wore rimless glasses which gave him the look of a professional civil servant, if you failed to look into his eyes, which gave no quarter and expected none except from a fool. I guess maybe he smiled once, about ten years ago.

It was the older one whose hand was raised in the act of knocking on the door.

"Pendrick Duggan?"

"The same."

"Compliments of the American ambassador, Mr. Duggan." They pulled out identical wallets with identical identification cards. I didn't get a chance to figure out the exact agency they belonged to before they flipped the wallets back into their pockets. "Your presence is required at the embassy."

"Sorry, gentlemen, I've got a meeting in a half-hour. Then a funeral to attend."

"You misunderstand the nature of this request, Mr. Duggan."

"You mean you have the authority to make the request stick." The older one nodded.

"Come in for a second." I looked outside, saw their car parked at the curb. It was an ordinary black Chev.

I thought about my pension for a moment. I picked up my suitcoat in my left hand, and the gun beneath it in my right.

"Okay, lads. Against the wall." Wearily, glancing at each other, they took up the position against the wall as if they had done it hundreds of times before. As a touch of politeness, I kicked their legs wider apart. Once more, they glanced at each other, but didn't say anything.

I pulled their wallets out, put them on the dining room table. They were each wearing a gun, which I also confiscated.

"Tsk, tsk, lads. I'd bet a million dollars you don't have any authorization to carry these in this country. Too bad. Okay, you can turn around now."

They turned around. "You've had your fun, Mr. Duggan. Now, let's go."

I scribbled my name and phone number on a slip of paper, not wavering the gun an inch. "If your ambassador wishes a meeting, I suggest he call me during business hours at this number." I handed the slip to the older one.

They were watching each other without seeming to. I could guess they were debating jumping me, trying to figure out if I would actually shoot in my own house. I certainly didn't want to.

I moved closer. "Carrying a concealed weapon is an indictable offence, gentlemen. Should you refuse to leave now, I would construe that as interfering in the activities of a law officer. Also an indictable offence." I handed each his wallet in turn. I didn't really care what their names were. "Now, please leave."

They stood still, staring pointedly at the two guns on the table. I put them in my jacket pocket.

"If you have legitimate claim to these items, present yourself at the police station tomorrow."

They left. They weren't too happy but they left. I thought even more about my pension.

I slipped into St. Brigid's just for a moment before getting started downtown. I lit a candle for my mother, said two quick Hail Marys and left quietly by the side entrance. In those days, church doors were open more often than not; today they always seem to be locked when a person wants to drop in for a minute. No wonder people don't go to church like they used to.

One thing that hasn't changed in thirty years is that the Party Palace has always served a good breakfast. Still does. I had a breakfast special with two eggs, Bruno had the special with four. Bruno was a big man.

I chatted him up about the case. He muttered every once in awhile. We lingered over coffee; lots of time yet before eight o'clock.

Bruno was full of good advice. He wouldn't have rough-housed the Russian. And he wouldn't have pulled a gun on the Americans.

To change the subject, I asked him how his parents were doing.

"Bah! Same as ever. First one dies, the other one's goin' back to Poland. They're each waitin' for the other to die so's they can go back home."

"Why don't they go back together?"

"Two reasons. First is, they didn't do so good over here, and they don't want to go back with their tails between their legs. Second, whoever dies, the other one will use the insurance money to pay the fare back."

"Bruno, it's gotta be better here, no matter what. Who'd want to go back to Poland? Poland stinks."

"You know it, I know it. To them, it's home. They'll go back there, they'll hate it. But every day they're here, they think about the old days, before the war, before the Nazis, and it gets better in their imagination every day."

Bruno was right. That's just human nature.

We walked up to Lyon Street and over to Turner's place. His wife offered coffee, but we were already overloaded. From there we went up to Somerset.

The owner of the apartment block was a small Jewish lady in her seventies. She didn't look pleased to see us.

"So it's taking three big policemen to ask questions of one small lady. For this I left Austria?" She glared belligerently at us. Bruno got the message and sent Turner with one of the photographs to canvass the neighbours.

We showed her the picture. "The lady in 4-B. So what has the poor girl done?"

"What makes you think she's done something?"

"You think all old ladies is dumb, I suppose. For two days she's not coming home and then three policemen come knocking on my door. So I'm supposed to think everything is normal, maybe?"

"Could you tell us the name of this lady?"

"Katrina."

"She got a last name?"

"You making fun of me? Of course she's got a last name. I don't know what it is, though."

"You'd rent an apartment to a lady, you don't even know her last name?"

She glared at Bruno like he was some sort of cockroach or something. "What are you saying? I didn't rent no apartment to her."

I was getting a bit exasperated, cute as she was. "Hold it, hold it. You just told us that this was a photo of the lady in apartment 4-B."

"Yes." More glaring.

"But you don't know her name."

"Yes."

"Yes, you know her name or yes you don't know her name?"

"God gave you ears to listen with, a brain to understand with. What's wrong with you, you don't understand."

"I pass. Bruno, you try."

"If you didn't rent the apartment to the lady, who did you rent it to?"

"A very nice gentleman, he was from the embassy. He rented it for this lady to live in."

"Could we see a copy of the lease, please?"

It was a lot of trouble for her to get the lease. She should be paid for her time. She had work to do, we wouldn't believe. But, finally, she produced a lease.

It was signed by Nikola Cherniak.

The young lady was quiet, always paid her rent on time. Not like some others she could mention. She didn't spy on her tenants, she didn't know anything about her personal life. There were no complaints about her from the other tenants. Not like those two men sharing apartment 4-C, the stories she could tell us about them.

We didn't have time to listen to stories about apartment 4-C, so we bade her farewell.

Incongruously, she waved, "Come again, anytime. Always glad to have visitors."

Turner was taking one side of the street, so Bruno took the other while I went after the tenants in the building. Most people were at work. The man in apartment 2-A admitted he was calling in sick today, even though he didn't feel too bad. He recognized the picture as "that Russian lady in 4-B. Good looker. Tried to talk to her a couple of times but she wasn't having any." He said this when his wife was out of earshot. He didn't have a name, but thought someone referred to her one time as Tina.

No one else knew anything, or if they did they weren't saying. I went looking for Bruno and Turner.

We met at the corner of Somerset and Bay. Turner was the only one who had had any luck. The guy at the corner grocery store knew her name was Tina, she was Russian, spoke very good English, was pretty, wasn't married, didn't date non-Russians, had been in Canada for six months, liked Montreal but wasn't too crazy about Ottawa and would like to be posted to Washington some day. Turner had all this written down in his notebook.

The best Bruno had done was find a lady who referred to her as that "foreign bitch," who she thought was making eyes at her husband. Since the husband was getting close to sixty, it didn't seem too likely.

Turner seemed to be having all the luck, so we left him to do some more canvassing. Bruno had to get back to the station, and I had a funeral to attend.

The funeral seemed like old home week. The Senator was there. Carson was there. Duckworth from External Affairs was there. The prime minister was there. The leader of the opposition was there. Members of parliament from both sides of the House were there. Diplomats by the limousine-full were there. No Russians, though. The funeral was held at St. Andrews Presbyterian Church at the corner of Kent Street and Wellington, in sight of Parliament Hill. It seemed like everything was happening in sight of that damned Peace Tower.

As we were dispersing after the service, I saw Duckworth making a bee-line for me. I tried to turn, but wasn't fast enough. He didn't look happy. He tried to whisper, but half the congregation could hear him. I saw Carson out of the corner of my eye watching us carefully. Duckworth grabbed my arm and gripped it tightly.

"Duggan!" I had been demoted from inspector. "What the hell do you think you're doing?"

I put on my most innocent face. "Doing?"

"I've had screaming Russians on my phone for half the morning. They're talking about diplomatic notes flying around my ear."

"As long as they're diplomatic."

"What?"

"The notes, I mean. Diplomatic. Not angry."

"I've got to get back to my office. We've got to talk. Later. I've got the Americans on my back, too, now. I've got three urgent phone messages to answer. I pray to God that's not you, too."

I silently guessed that God wasn't going to answer his prayers. I said I'd call him a bit later. He stalked off, nodding and smiling to all the diplomats.

Mrs. Robinson gave me a glance as she was getting into her limousine. I nodded. Carson was making his way towards me in a casual, but deliberate, manner. He was in Class-A uniform.

"Mornin', Duggan."

"Top o' the mornin', Sergeant. Looks like the weather might break."

"Just might, Detective." The limousines going to the cemetery were pulling away.

"Pretty uniforms you Mounties wear."

"Tradition."

"Saw the Musical Ride one time. Impressive."

"Tried out for it when I was a young buck. Wasn't a good enough rider."

"Just as well. It's a rough life, showbiz."

"Yeah. So, what's new?"

"I was hoping to ask you that. I've had nothing but disappointment and dead ends."

"Sometimes it gets like that. Find out who the dead lady is yet?"

"You could be right, Carson. Might be Voscovitch. Not sure yet, but her first name seems to be Katrina or Tina."

"Tina's probably a contraction of Katrina." We started walking up Wellington towards Mountie headquarters.

"Yeah, that's what I thought. Bet you'll never guess who signed the lease for her apartment."

"You're probably right. I'm lousy at guessing games."

"That Russian translator, Nikola Cherniak."

"How convenient." We had arrived at the justice building.

"You may recall he said he never saw the dead girl before."

"Now that you remind me, I do recall."

"I suppose he's got diplomatic immunity."

"I would imagine so."

"Might chat him up a bit, anyway."

"Let me know how it turns out." He turned to enter his headquarters.

"You and me and the Senator going to get together someday soon?"

"Good idea. I'll try to set it up. I'll call you later."

"Good. Leave a message if I'm not in."

"It's nice working with you, Duggan." His smile seemed genuine.

"Same for me, Carson." He went inside, I walked up the street.

I got as far as the Windsor Hotel on Queen Street. The Windsor was across the street from the Ottawa *Citizen* newspaper. I rationalized that I might meet somebody useful and stepped inside for a quick one.

The Windsor was full of the noontime crowd. Mostly civil servants drinking their lunch. At one table, a few *Citizen* workers.

I sat down, ordered a couple of drafts. It was only then that I saw old Bill making his way towards me. If I had seen him first, I wouldn't have come in.

Bill sat down uninvited. "Spare the cost of a beer, Pendrick?" Sighing, I ordered Bill a couple. At least it was company.

"Long time no see, Pendrick. How's things?"

"Not too bad. And you?"

"Same as ever. Days are long. Too long."

I had met old Bill overseas. He had been an engineer in Canada before the war. Over there they had him blowing up bridges instead of building them. He was older than most of the fellows in his outfit so, at the grand old age of twenty-six, he became 'old' Bill.

When he came home, something happened. He hit the bottle too hard, split up with his wife, alienated his family, and ended up on skid row, or what passed in Ottawa for skid row. He was a bum.

"Got anything I should know?" Bill had a sharp eye sometimes, and on occasion I slipped him a few bucks for information.

"Not a goddamned thing." He was on his second draft. I ordered four more.

"Well, maybe next time, Bill." I could smell the stale vomit and urine coming off him. I hoped he'd leave soon, and that he wouldn't start any of his bloody reminiscing. I always liked old Bill, but sometimes he was a pain in the ass.

No such luck. He eyed me tearfully over the rim of his glass. "I was a good soldier, wasn't I, Pendrick? A good soldier."

"You were a good soldier, Bill. A good soldier."

"Damned right, I was. Damned right." As usual, he made a production of pulling an old leather wallet from his back pocket. From it, he extracted a sheaf of faded, yellowed papers. "See this, Pendrick? My discharge papers. Honourable Discharge. See here? See this newspaper article? It shows all the medals I won. I got a goddamned honourable discharge from the goddamned army. I fought for my goddamned country. Not like a lot of these cowards around here." He glared around belligerently.

"Not now, Bill. Don't start anything."

"Why not, Pendrick, why not?" He clambered unsteadily to his feet, waving his papers. "At least I wasn't afraid to go fight for my country. Not like the bunch of zombies sitting here today."

Bill had gone too far, and there were murmurs of dissent from several tables. Zombies were men who had not volunteered for overseas duty in the war. Nobody liked to think of himself as a zombie, even if he was one. Somebody told Bill to shut the fuck up. I pulled him down on his seat. I knew as long as I sat there, nobody would make trouble for Bill.

Except the waiter. He came over and lifted Bill bodily from his chair. "Out. Right now. Get out and don't come back. You're barred." He began hustling Bill towards the back door.

"Ask Pendrick. He knows I'm right. Don't you, Pendrick?" Bill was in tears now, shovelling the papers back into his wallet. "An honourable discharge." I knew that as soon as he got to the bottom of the back stairs he would forget his humiliation and head for the next bar.

I always liked Bill. I don't know what happened to him after the war.

The beer suddenly tasted flat. I took off my tie and made my way out the door.

I headed downtown to visit Luc Gerrard. He was the guy who had first discovered the body of the girl in the park.

Gerrard worked in one of the temporary buildings. The temporary buildings had been built for wartime use, but they were still here. Probably will still be here long after the Parliament Buildings have fallen.

He thought it was terrible that someone would kill a girl in one of Ottawa's beautiful parks, and wondered what the city was coming to. I wondered right along with him.

He was walking to the bus stop on Laurier Avenue when he saw the girl. At first, he thought she might have fallen and hit her head, knocking herself out. It was only when he leaned down to look at her that he knew she was dead.

He hadn't seen anyone in the park, nor on the street. Now that he thought about it, maybe there was one man walking west on Laurier. Away from the Russian Embassy.

Apart from that, he knew nothing. He thought the police should have more patrolmen on duty. Also that we were letting too many foreigners into the country. He was a pain in the ass, especially considering he was working for the immigration department, which was letting all those foreigners in.

I thanked him politely and turned to leave. Just loud enough so that all the secretaries who were trying to listen to our conversation could hear, I informed Mr. Gerrard that he had convinced me that he had nothing to do with the crime and that I was just doing my duty in questioning him. All the secretaries pretended they hadn't heard me, but they'd be gossiping and speculating for days. Serve Gerrard right.

I grabbed a streetcar back to the station.

Nikola Cherniak wasn't in when I called. I left a message. I asked around for Turner, but he hadn't reported in yet. I was at loose ends a bit, so I just sat back and mulled over what I knew.

The phone rang. It was Duckworth.

"Tell me this, Duggan: have you beaten up a Russian, got two other Russians down to the police station to view the dead body of a person they've never seen before, and held two American agents at gunpoint, confiscating their weapons?"

I admitted the truth of all that.

"My God, Duggan."

I was getting a bit tired of Duckworth's attitude. "To you, it's Mister Duggan, or Detective Duggan. Mister Duckworth."

"Sorry about that. But you don't realize! You don't have the power to do things like that."

"It's you that doesn't realize. First, if any Russian wants to press charges against me for assault, let him do that. If those two assholes still insist the body they were forced to see is not Katrina Voscovitch, let them put that on paper. Preferably in a diplomatic note. Third, if those Americans can prove ownership and the right to carry their pistols, they can pick them up at the station tomorrow. When I'm on a murder investigation, it doesn't matter to me if it's Canadians or Americans or Russians who are the killers."

"I thought we were talking suicide here."

"I did mention a second body to you the other night. You're putting two cases together. I'm talking about a dead body that has every indication of being a Russian body."

"How do you know that?"

"Tell you the truth, I'd know a lot more if those Russians would cooperate. Right now, I'm just trying to identify the body, I'm not even working on finding whoever killed her. Of course, the longer it takes to identify her, the longer time the killer has to get away."

"A Russian murdered? In Ottawa? I find that hard to believe."

"Believe it or not." I wasn't giving him anything.

"Why assault a Russian chauffeur? You think he did the murder?"

"I didn't like his attitude."

"Being smart-ass won't get us anywhere, Detective." He had moved me upward a notch again.

"Sorry. I'm tired, and my body aches, and I've got two cases on my hands, and I'm not getting anywhere on either one of them. I get testy sometimes."

"I should say! Okay, let's leave the Russian chauffeur for a moment. What's the story about the American agents?"

"That one's easier. They were carrying concealed weapons, which is against the law in Ottawa."

"For God's sake, Detective! We're talking about official government agents."

"Agents of a foreign power."

"Well, technically."

"Technically or not, they were breaking the law, and I had no recourse but to step in. Any other action would be considered dereliction of duty."

"You're playing games now, Detective, and my department takes a dim view."

"You're right. But I might have fewer games to play if I received any cooperation in my investigations."

He sighed deeply. "All right, Detective Duggan. How may the Department of External Affairs assist you in your investigations?"

"I thought you'd never ask. How's about I visit you in your office in about a half an hour?"

"I'll see you, Detective." He hung up abruptly. He didn't seem too pleased at the prospect.

It was my day for phone calls. I hate phones, and normally I avoid them as much as possible, but sometimes there's no escape. This was a good one, though. It was Lukowicz.

"Detective, I've made a call or two on your behalf."

"Nice of you to help out, Ed." I waited for the explanation.

"How would you like to have a word or two with Igor Gouzenko?" I almost dropped the phone.

In my mind, I could see his smile as he asked the innocent question. I had one to match on my face. "You really mean it?"

"Yep. I made a coupla calls to some of my old buddies, explained the situation, and made a deal."

"I owe you one."

"More than you'll ever know."

"Where? When? How?"

"Get right to the point, don't you? Okay, here's what's happening. We're gonna catch the train to Toronto tomorrow, check in at the Royal York Hotel. Someone will phone us there, set up a meet. Don't know where or when yet."

"Real cloak and dagger stuff."

"Yeah, well, that's Gouzenko all the way. He loves this sort of stuff. Prob'ly that's why he agreed to meet us."

We arranged to meet in time to catch the seven a.m. train to Toronto. I was glad Lukowicz was coming along. "Ed, thanks a lot. This might be a wild goose chase, you know."

"Oh I know, in fact I expect it. But still, it's good to be back in harness again. I haven't had so much excitement in two years. I love it."

I called in on Duckworth. I was kept in a waiting room for about ten minutes. Keeping me in my place. But I was in a good mood for a change, so it didn't bother me.

After I was waved into his office, he sent his secretary out for a coffee and a tea. He looked tense behind a large desk piled with papers. He cleared an area, brought out a legal-sized yellow pad, went to a pencil-sharpener on the windowsill, sharpened two pencils, held one in his hand ready to write and placed the second alongside the pad. He was left-handed.

He smiled. "I was posted to Cairo once. Seems I spent half my time there dealing with police officials about one thing or another. Haven't had an occasion since coming to Ottawa. It's never easy. Someone's always in trouble."

I agreed it probably was never easy. His secretary brought in the tea and coffee. I was surprised; she had made the tea in a little china teapot. It was still weak, but it tasted good. I let it steep for awhile.

"Well, Mr. Duckworth, where do we start?"

"Well, Detective." He had the start of a smile on his face again. "Why not pretend we've never met before. You tell me the story so far, and see where External Affairs can assist you in your investigations."

"Very civilized, I like that."

I told him most of everything, leaving out only the phone call from the woman I believed to be Katrina Voscovitch.

Duckworth looked stunned. "So, where do we begin?"

"Tell me all about how your security clearance system works."

He cleared his throat, threw down his pencil. The tip broke on the desk. "You've come to the heart of the friction between External and the Mounted Police. The Mounties do the actual security check of our employees, and have the right to recommend that we refuse employment if they find anything suspicious in their character. It's a real pain in the ass, because we disagree so often.

"The Mounties have two fixed ideas about subversives: that they consist of 'commies and queers', as they so gently put it. As far as the first is concerned, if your great-grandmother came from Lithuania, they're convinced the whole family is a nest of communist sympathizers. As for the second, they're convinced anyone not married by age twenty-five is at least a latent homosexual."

I put down my cup. "You know I'm cooperating with the Mounties in this case. I bet they've got a different version of that."

"So right. They think this whole department is run directly from Moscow. They get exasperated sometimes."

"So, tell me about the two security clearances for Robinson."

"Three, actually."

"Three? Good Lord, how many times does a man have to prove his innocence?"

"It's not a matter of innocence or guilt. In security, no one is actually ever charged with anything. Well, hardly ever, only if he's actually been caught giving away or selling state secrets. And, even then, if it would be too embarrassing to the government, he might only be dismissed, not charged."

"I can see that."

"So, it's really a matter of innuendo, hearsay, suspicion, gossip that can ruin a man's career." He still had not written a word. He stood up, walked to the window-ledge and re-sharpened his pencil.

"Or a woman's."

"Yes, of course." He sat again.

"Back to Robinson. Three investigations. Seems excessive."

"The first time was just routine. That was when he was recruited into the service. The foreign service, that is. I recommended him, his family looked okay, he went to good schools, was bright, articulate, all the right things. As a security clearance, it really was quite superficial.

"You see, it wasn't until the Gouzenko mess that we really got serious about subversion."

I was surprised at the mention of Gouzenko again that day. I hoped it didn't tell on my face.

"The first real investigation was the result of peculiar circumstances. Robinson had been in Washington during the war, then he was posted to Cracow, Poland, as a sort of cultural affairs officer. He had an expert knowledge of chess, you know."

"He wrote a couple of books, I believe."

"That's right. It was thought that his chess skill would give him entrée into certain groups, invitations to tournaments, that sort of thing."

"Makes sense. Eastern Europeans are all chess fanatics, I've heard."

"Yes, well. After a few years, we decided to post him to New York, to the United Nations. We submitted his name to the Americans for accreditation. They denied it.

"We were shocked, asked why. It seemed his name appeared on a secret list of possible subversives.

"It didn't make any sense to us, but we went through a serious investigation anyway."

"Done by Sergeant Carson."

"It's actually a group of people, but Carson was part of it."

"They didn't find anything."

"Carson was convinced Robinson was a security risk, but he couldn't find any proof. He recommended he be dismissed. We overruled him.

"However, we still couldn't send him into the States, so he was posted to Australia."

I finished my tea, stood up and paced across his floor. "Okay, next investigation."

"Years later, it crops up again. The House Un-American Activities Committee names him as a subversive, claims he's being sheltered by the State Department, smears his name all over the papers, and asks him to come down and testify."

"So, again, we investigate. This is only three weeks ago. We recall him to Ottawa and put him through extreme grilling, total investigation back to the womb.

"Once again, Carson is convinced he's a communist, but can't find a shred of evidence."

"Carson seemed to be trying to convince me he wasn't a communist, but that he had some acquaintances who were."

"To the Mounties, that's the same thing. It means you're unreliable."

"Could I see the reports on Robinson?"

Duckworth pushed his seat back. He looked glum. "That

would be against every rule we have. You couldn't even subpoena those reports." I said nothing. He rose, walked around the desk and riffled through a stack of files. "I don't have a copy of the current report. Here's the one done in 1949. You can't leave the office with it. I'll go for a walk. Be back in twenty minutes." He closed the door gently behind him.

I opened the report, not sure what I was looking for. I began reading. The first thing that struck me was the immensity of the resources the Mounties were able to put into their investigation. It fairly took away the breath of a small-town cop. School records, interviews with grade-school teachers, part-time employers, parents, friends of parents, college professors, acquaintances in Canada, the States and England. Now, that's investigation. A person couldn't hide too much after a grilling like that.

But is seemed Robinson was as clean as a guy could be in his mid-thirties. There was a bit about cheating on an old exam, a bit about a former schoolmate and friend who had been jailed on assault charges. There was a spot of financial difficulty in England, leading to a possible lawsuit until Robinson paid up.

And then there were the innuendo, hearsay, suspicion and gossip which Duckworth had mentioned. As a child, he wasn't athletic, but studious. Several of his Cambridge friends were "artists." Hence, suspicion. Against that was the fact he was married. But against that was the fact that he didn't have any children. Hell. Why didn't they just ask his wife if he was queer or not? A professor at Cambridge was considered to be a Marxist. During an interview with the Mounties he had used the word "proletariat." His views were decidedly anti-German, not simply anti-Nazi.

His wife had been investigated also. Her background, back through grade school, was laid out on paper. The conclusion on her was that she was apolitical, but trouble could be anticipated because of undocumented stories of various love affairs both before and after her marriage.

There were amazing leaps to unverifiable conclusions. The report suggested it was possible that Robinson may have joined a Marxist reading group at Cambridge (the writer had the grace to admit that Robinson denied this). It further stated that, despite his marriage, Robinson's sexuality was questionable. It concluded that, because of this and because of his wife's reputed affairs, Robinson might be a possible target for blackmail by an unspecified foreign power.

In conclusion, the report recommended that Robinson's security clearance be revoked and that he be dismissed.

The next few pages contained External Affairs' response. Seven different people, including the minister, recommended rejection of the report's conclusions. Interestingly, not one of them based their recommendations on rejection of the Mounties' allegations, but only on the fact that the suspicions were too vague and undocumented to be taken seriously "at this time."

What a nice bunch. They wouldn't throw the poor devil to the wolves today. Nothing about tomorrow, though.

I was rereading the file when Duckworth returned. "Learn anything?"

"Yeah. I wouldn't want the boys in red doing one of those investigations on me."

He smiled ruefully. "I was put through it once. As I understand it, they found something out about me that made them hesitate. That was ten years ago, and to this day I still can't find out what it was."

"I appreciate the looksee at this. Is there anything else you can tell me about Robinson?"

"Nothing that you don't know already."

"Robinson had a lot of visitors to his hotel room the week before he died. Was that your fellows?"

"More likely Carson's."

"Okay. A new tack. How does the Senator fit into all this?"

"Why do you ask?"

"I understand he also made a few visits."

Duckworth leaned back in his chair, sucking the end of his pencil. He threw it down on the desk. The tip broke again. "I didn't know that."

"I take it you're upset because that means there's a few other things you probably don't know."

He tried to smile. "Things I probably should know. The Senator goes way back in politics. That's one of the disadvantages of having the same ruling party for the best part of this century. The old boys hang around for an awfully long time."

"Even longer than the civil servants sometimes."

"Yeah. Well, the Senator prides himself on knowing every dirty little secret this town has, as well as a lot more in Montreal and Quebec City. He believes that knowledge is power, and that knowledge of other people's sins is even more power."

"Now, that's interesting. The Senator's own background is not that clean."

"If the wrong person ever heard you say that, you'd be off the force tomorrow. Within a month you'd be a broken, financially ruined, humbled man with a bewildered look on your face."

I'm afraid my pride got the better of me. I laughed. "Me and the Senator. Now, by Jesus, that would be a truly great donnybrook."

"Don't laugh, Detective. I've seen him do it before. And to men who thought they had incredible power. Members of Parliament. A speaker of the House. A former judge. He can be ruthless."

"Of that I've no doubt, lad. But, still, it would be great fun. However, it doesn't answer my question. What was his interest in Robinson?"

"I'm not sure. I would imagine he was keeping tabs on the investigation, on behalf of the prime minister. If Robinson had dirty secrets to tell the Americans that even the P.M. didn't know about, it could cause great trouble. Even bring down the government."

"I suppose it could be as simple as that. I guess it's just the Senator's character, or lack of it, that makes me wonder."

"I can see you getting in trouble on this one, Detective. My advice would be to leave the Senator alone."

"Oh, you're right, lad, right as rain. Let's change the subject and concentrate on another corpse for the moment.

"Let us assume that the dead woman is this Voscovitch person. What would the Russians gain by denying it, and could they get away with it?"

"Two different questions. The answer to the first is I don't know and the answer to the second is yes."

"Surely when she came into the country she had to register somewhere. Wouldn't there be a description, fingerprints, and all that?"

"It sounds so simple, but the truth is, no. She would have come in on a diplomatic passport. She's registered, all right, but that wouldn't help you identify your corpse."

"Can we compel them to produce this Katrina person, if they insist she's not dead?"

"If we were sure of our facts we could. But all you have so far is suspicion. One convincingly denied by the Soviets. Nobody would authorize such a demand."

"Jesus, but you fellows make a policeman's lot a hard one. Let's try a hypothetical question. If Canada were sure this Katrina was a Soviet spy, would our security forces have the authority to kill her?"

"Unlike the Soviet Union, all persons in this country, citizen or not, have the same rights. The plain answer is no. She could be expelled from the country. All Canadians she might have implicated could be prosecuted. But nobody has the power to murder."

"What you mean is nobody has the authorization. Lots of people have the power."

"A subtle distinction."

"I'm a subtle man." That got the biggest smile yet out of Duckworth. "Okay, let's move to your complaint number two against me. Two Americans, agents of some agency or other, waving guns and inviting me to a friendly chat with their ambassador. How about them having some reason to kill Katrina?"

"Your guess is as good as mine. Doesn't seem likely, though. And before you ask it, no, they couldn't possibly have any authorization for a killing, at least not Canadian authorization. And it's highly unlikely they'd commit such an act in a friendly country. In East Germany, that might be a different story."

I was pacing again. "Which brings us back to the Soviets again."

"For what reason?"

"If I knew that, me lad, I'd know a lot more than I do now, that's for sure. Goddammit. My head is hurting me."

Duckworth sharpened his pencil again. He looked like he would like to pace too, but there wasn't room enough in the office for both of us to pace.

"Well Mr. Duckworth, I'm going to let it rest for now. I'll no doubt be in touch later. As for your concerns, I repeat what I said this morning. I deny using excessive force on the chauffeur. Let him try to prove it. I am convinced the dead girl is Voscovitch and I would welcome an official written Soviet denial. And, I was within my legal rights to confiscate the weapons of the American nationals."

"Well, Detective, now you're the one making a diplomat's lot a hard one. I'll make as many soothing noises as I can, but I sincerely hope you terminate your investigation soon. We prefer smoothness and quietness."

I had no doubt they did. So did I, come to think of it.

I walked back to the station. Perhaps it was my imagination, but I thought it was getting a bit cooler.

The Chief was not in a good mood. I could hear him yelling at some hapless constable over the phone even before he opened his door to let me in.

For once, I told the truth. I said I was off to Toronto for the day on a wild goose chase.

The Chief yelled at me for awhile. Then he agreed to a deal. If it was a wild goose chase, I'd pay for the trip out of my own pocket. If it produced some results, the city would pay.

Some deal.

I phoned Carson to say I'd be out of town tomorrow and to ask him to set up the meeting with the Senator on my return.

Carson was glad to do it. He didn't ask me where I was going. That should have told me something.

CHAPTER 10

It was ironic that the most convenient spot for Ed and me to meet was the lobby of the Chateau Laurier. From there we could take the underground tunnel to the Union Station across Wellington Street to catch our train to Toronto. We wouldn't have to come out into daylight again until after we had checked into our hotel room in Toronto, for there was another tunnel connecting the Toronto Union Station with the Royal York Hotel. Those days of convenience and service are now long gone. More's the pity.

Ed had on a checked sport coat that made him look even smaller than I remembered him, but he had a wide smile on his face as he came bounding into the lobby. He, at least, was prepared for fun. I was wearing only a short-sleeved shirt. My jacket was packed away. It felt like a school holiday. Ed's grin was infectious.

I bought the tickets and we settled in for the ride. We didn't talk until the train was well into the countryside. Ed pulled out a cribbage board and a deck of cards. The steward set up a table for us. He smiled a lot.

Ed broke the silence as he shuffled the cards. "Been to Toronto much?"

I cut. A seven of hearts. "Twice. Not my favourite town."

Ed cut a three of diamonds. He won first deal. "Know what you mean. Protestant town. Methodists, Baptists, Anglicans and Orangemen. Not a jolly city."

I surveyed my hand, kept an eight-point hand, a run of three and a pair. I gave Ed a seven and an eight. It was only the first hand.

Unfortunately, Ed threw in a six and a nine, then I cut another six for him. Fourteen points in the crib alone. It was going to be a long ride to Toronto. Especially at a penny a point.

I watched the countryside pass and tried to distract Ed with chit-chat. "Hear you have to be an Orangeman to get a job with the Toronto police force. Any truth in that?"

"Might be something to it. Probably an exaggeration, though."

"You belong to any societies, lodges, things like that?"

"Not me. The force frowns on secret societies. I suppose you belong to the Knights of Columbus."

I admitted the truth of that. "Don't participate much, though. Pay my dues, show up at the odd communion breakfast. Not a very secret society, the Knights."

Sometimes, even while I'm talking my mind wanders. I remember when I was a little kid, the annual twelfth of July Orange parade was a big event in Lowertown. There were floats and bands and marchers and banners. Everyone came out to line the streets to watch, even devout Catholics. It was a change from everyday boredom.

I remember particularly one parade when I was five or six years old. One of the floats was a shameless attack on the Catholic church. High up on a plywood throne was a man dressed as the pope, with mitre and cape. Below him on the flatbed of the truck was a herd of pigs. The "pope" was throwing hosts to his "congregation" of pigs.

Young as I was, I was outraged. I started yelling and screaming and crying.

My mother's strong right hand swept across the back of my head and knocked me to the sidewalk. "Keep quiet or go inside." I sniffled for awhile, but watched the rest of the parade. I didn't understand.

In our house, every Saturday night was party night and the kitchen and parlour would be filled with relatives and friends. Eventually, the talk would get around to "The Troubles", and stories of great deeds by Irish Catholic patriots against Orangemen and Englishmen would be told embellished with the re-telling. Someone would start a slow, sad song of defiance and rebellion, and soon the house was filled with the sound of half-drunken Irish voices weaving in and out of unsure harmony.

Ed grunted as he threw down his sixteen-point hand, smiling. "I never can understand your Irish feuds."

Neither can I.

We rolled leisurely through the lush Ontario countryside, both of us marvelling at the sense of permanent prosperity portrayed by the fields of corn waving high in the sun, vegetable gardens in ripe, orderly rows, rolling green pastures and fat herds of lazy cattle.

I threw a blank crib down in disgust. "Makes a city boy yearn for the country life."

"Fifteen two, fifteen four, fifteen six, fifteen eight, a pair is ten and another pair is twelve." Ed totalled the new score. I owed him over five dollars, and we still had two hours to go. "Too much work for me. I like living in the country, but you'd never find me working a farm."

I agreed. When my ancestors had come to Canada, they had settled in various parts of the Ottawa Valley, all taking up farming and logging. Within a generation, the sons and daughters had drifted to the bigger towns and cities. Now we were definitely an urban family. I could dream of the country, but I'd never really go to live there. Of course, when I was a kid, you could live in the city and still keep a garden; during the Depression, it was a practical necessity. But those days were fast disappearing. Now they're gone altogether.

Lunchtime came, and we were served a delicious meal in the sparkling dining car. I owed Ed enough to pay for his lunch. I never was that good in cribbage. Euchre was my game.

Ed was napping when the train slowed down as it entered Toronto. I nudged him, and we pressed our noses against the window like a couple of kids.

I thought that there must be more scenic ways to enter a city. We passed what seemed to be miles and miles of run-down slums. I took them to be the famous Cabbagetown, but I wasn't sure. Neither was Ed. He thought it might be the Corktown ghetto. Following that, we passed what seemed to be miles and miles of industrial warehousing served by the railway and the ships on Lake Ontario.

Ed shook his head and asked, smiling, "Howdja like to be a cop here?"

"Argh. I'm sure it would break my heart. Makes Lowertown look like Park Avenue. Still and all, I went to New York City only once in my life, and the slums there're even worse. And all full of coloured people. Now, that's a place I would hate to patrol dressed in blue."

Ed straightened his tie and pulled on his jacket as we rolled towards Union Station. "The government is pulling down all the slums, and replacing them with new apartments. They call it Regent Park. Fancy name. You hear funny stories about how all them people fit in."

"Well, people is the same anywhere, lad. Seems to me, if they kept their house neat and tidy, they'll do the same with their new apartments. If not...well, what can you do?"

We stood and collected our hand luggage. "I went to a conference once, and they described Cabbagetown as the largest Anglo-Saxon slum in the world. Most slums're made up of recent immigrants, coloured, that sort. Cabbagetown is all English and Scottish. Poor people, but the right sort." He slapped me on the back. "That's where your Orange Lodge rules. God Save the King, down with the Pope, vote for George Drew, all that."

"My favourite type of people." Ed laughed.

We pulled into the station. Toronto. The adventure begins.

We bought a bottle of whiskey at the liquor store in the tunnel, then walked across to the Royal York. We checked into a double room and sat down to wait.

We were waiting for a "Mister Brown" to call us and make an appointment. Ed told me that was Gouzenko's favourite alias. "Inventive," I grunted. We poured a couple of tumblers of the whiskey. I was used to sitting and waiting. I supposed Ed must be too.

After about three hours, Mister Brown called. He had a hoarse voice, with a strong accent. He informed us that he would come to our room in a half-hour.

I rubbed my hands together and paced the floor, sipping my whiskey. Ed stretched out on one of the beds.

Suddenly, he leapt up and stood looking out the window. He was as anxious as me. "Don't expect too much," he cautioned. "It's been nine years since this guy has had anything to do with spies and all that. How can he remember that far back?"

I smiled. "You never know. Apart from memory, there's always stories, rumours, myths."

"Myths?"

"Yeah. Nobody really knows all the facts, but there's always stories floating about, no names, just a story about one time long ago when, maybe, let's make up something, there was this hit man that came into town from Chicago and he did away with this bootlegger, but then he fell in love with the guy's wife and stole her away to Chicago in a blaze of gunfire when her brothers found out what was happening. Now, lad, the thing is, the story has been told over and over again, and been exaggerated and distorted, but underneath all of that, there's a kernel of truth about, maybe, a guy from Chicago who took the bootlegger's wife back home with him. That could be the part of the story you're interested in, that might lead to the solution of a case that's got nothing to do with bootleggers and killers." I laughed harshly. "There probably never was a hit-man, and the wife probably went to Chicago willingly, and there never was any gunfire. But nobody ever lets facts get in the way of a good story."

"And you want to hear a myth about a shadowy diplomat who was the secret mastermind of a spy ring for twenty years, and he gave the intelligence unit fits trying to figure out who he was, and he gave the atomic secrets to the Russians from right under the noses of the Mounted Police and MI5 and the CIA, laughing all the while." Ed's smile was wide as he pulled on his whiskey.

"Something like that. That story's a bit exaggerated, but I'll settle for any story that's got a diplomat and an American security committee and a Cambridge connection. Any story at all."

An hour passed, and no Mister Brown. The phone rang again.

Mr. Brown regretted he would be unable to attend the meeting as planned. Perhaps another time.

I get angry too fast. I blew my stack, telling him I had come three hundred miles for a meeting, and I wanted a bloody meeting. Mr. Brown did not reply.

Ed took the phone and, with his hand over the speaker, asked to give it a try, he knew what buttons to push.

"Mr. Brown, this is Mr. Lukowicz. I understand we have difficulties arranging a meeting. I wish to inform you that this is a matter of national urgency. While there can be no question of remuneration," – he winked at me – "there would be, of course, the gratitude of the entire Canadian nation." He was putting it on a bit thick, I thought.

There was a lot of talking back and forth, until Ed finally slammed the phone down on the receiver. I poured him a new drink. He mumbled to himself, walking back and forth, finally gulping the drink down and sitting on the bed. He ran his fingers through his thinning hair.

"Well?" I asked, running out of patience.

"Well, I've done the best I could. I maybe forgot to tell you that Gouzenko and the Mounties don't exactly get along too well."

"Can't you guys get along with anyone?"

"What do you mean?"

"Never mind. What did he say?"

"Okay. I'm out of it. He doesn't trust me. At nine o'clock tonight, you sit in the lobby of the hotel. Wear a shirt and tie, and hold your jacket over your lap. If someone asks you if you are "Mister Smith", agree that you are, and go off with him."

"Aw, nuts. This is cock-eyed."

Ed agreed. "It was the best I could do. If he shows up, he shows up. If not, we've wasted a trip out here."

"Hell. I'm not wasting this trip. If he doesn't show up, you can take me out to his house, and I'll rip him out of bed and make him talk."

"Sorry, Pen, I couldn't do that. If he doesn't show, it's all over."

I grumbled, but knew he was right. We had a few hours to kill, so we discussed eating.

Ed was enthusiastic. "How about Chinese? We could go down

to Chinatown." I hemmed and hawed, and finally had to admit I had never eaten Chinese food before.

I was mildly insulted by Ed's laughter. "What are you, forty-five years old? And you've never eaten Chinese! Come on, let's go, this will be a great adventure."

We hailed a cab and asked to be taken to Chinatown. Ed chortled most of the trip. "Never ate Chinese, I don't believe it! There's Chinese restaurants in Ottawa, at least four of 'em on Albert Street."

I squirmed. "Yeah, I just never had the occasion."

Ed snorted. "Occasion! I suppose you've eaten Italian food?"

"Yeah. I eat at Imbro's all the time. I like Italian."

"And French?"

"I was in France for part of the war."

"Well, Chinese is the third great cuisine in the world. You're gonna love it!"

The cab turned down Elizabeth Street, and Ed had him pass several of the fancy restaurants, and picked a small upstairs one near the bottom of the street. I was not impressed by the decor.

I let Ed order the food, and announced I would pass on the chopsticks. A knife and fork had suited me all my life, it was good enough now.

Ed was right. I loved it. I didn't know what I was eating for most of the meal, and knew better than to ask.

I patted my stomach as we sipped tea. I even bought two cheap cigars at the front counter, and we puffed contentedly. "I'm normally a meat and potatoes man, but that was good."

"Of course it's good. Eight hundred million people with a civilization thousands of years old have got to have learned a thing or two about cooking food."

We chatted about police matters for awhile. I asked Ed a question that had puzzled me for years. "Ed, I never arrested a Chinaman in more than twenty years on the force. What makes them so law-abiding?"

Ed was in a pontificating mood. "It comes from their culture, their respect for the family and the community. That's why I think they took to communism like a duck to water. There's so many of 'em, the actions of each individual affects the whole community more than here, so they're quick to punish the outlaw, even the free-thinker. After thousands of years, it's an ingrained part of their nature." He puffed contentedly on his stogie. "Mind you, you get a fair-sized Chinatown like here and Vancouver, there's crime all right, only the police never get to hear about it. It stays in the community, and they take care of their own problems."

"What kind of crime?"

"Well, there's lots of gambling goes on. Nobody complains about it, but I understand a Chinaman will gamble on most anything. There's more money lost and won every night in this neighbourhood than you or me'll ever see in our lifetime, that's for sure. Then there's the dope trade. Again, so long as it stays in Chinatown and doesn't get into the white neighbourhoods, the police never find out a thing about it. And then, there's extortion. Lots of gangs around, and lots of money changes hands so places don't burn down, so people don't fall down stairs, that kind of thing."

"Protection."

"Yeah. And the victims don't trust the police to be able to help them. Hell, most of them can't even speak English, so how can they complain, anyway?"

I wondered if Ed's knowledge was learned first-hand in the Mounties or gleaned from books. I felt better not knowing.

We paid our bill and cabbed back to the Royal York. I wanted an hour to think about meeting Mr. Brown.

At nine o'clock I was sitting in the lobby with my jacket on my lap. I felt foolish. At nine-thirty I started imagining that the clerks and bellmen were giving me suspicious looks. At ten o'clock I cursed myself for a fool, and swore I was leaving any minute. At ten-thirty, a shadow fell across me and a heavily-accented voice asked if I was Mister Smith.

I admitted I was and pointedly looked at my watch as I stood up. "Mr. Brown?" We shook hands. I looked him over. He was small, much smaller than I expected after hearing all the stories about him. He looked Slavic, all angles and squares. He really looked like someone type-cast by Hollywood to be a Russian. He was dressed in unpressed pants and baggy jacket.

We opted for the small bar next to the Imperial Room. I bought the drinks. I thought we looked incongruous, but shrugged, hoping we looked like two businessmen fixing up a deal. We probably looked exactly like what we were: a policeman and his informer.

I offered some chitchat about the weather. He wasn't interested. He informed me quickly that we was used to being paid for his time, and could spare very little of it. I told him there was a chance he could provide me with information regarding a man who might have been involved with Soviet intelligence in some way. He warmed to that, almost preening in self-importance.

I told him the story of Walter Robinson, adding all the conjectural possibilities I could think of. I asked him to search his memory for any information he might have.

He started talking. He told me his life story. He told me how the Soviet intelligence system works. He told me the tale of his defection. He confessed his fears that the Mounties were infiltrated by the KGB. He said the Soviets were still trying to find his identity and whereabouts so they could kill him. He was fascinating, and I quickly warmed to him. He informed me that he was one of the most important political figures of the twentieth century. He berated the Canadian government for not appreciating him more and providing for his financial well-being.

But not a word about Walter Robinson.

I moved closer. I asked a dozen questions. It was becoming obvious he didn't know anything that might help me, but I wasn't going to give up. Not after coming this far.

"There's got to be some connection with somebody in External Affairs." I was almost pleading by this time. Gouzenko looked blank. He sipped at his drink. He played with the paper napkin.

"There is Emma, of course."

"Emma?"

"Emma Voiken. She was in External Affairs. She was convicted and sentenced for two years."

"She knew Robinson?"

Gouzenko shrugged.

"Then there was that Willsher woman. She worked for the British High Commission."

"Is there a Robinson connection in that?" He shrugged elegantly once more. I sighed. I had come two hundred and fifty miles for this?

"There was the British scientist. His name is May... Allan Nunn May, as I recall. He is still in jail in England, I believe." He smiled softly.

"But you don't remember anything about a Canadian diplomat being involved anywhere?"

He turned a world-weary smile on me. Slowly, he shook his head. "So many, so very many," he mumbled into his drink.

"Well, I'll look into those three names, but..." I was feeling very discouraged.

"They pretend...," he mumbled into his drink.

"What's that?"

"Pretend to believe me. But they don't really want to."

"Who's pretending?"

"The government. The Mounties. They don't want to know." I was getting irritated.

"But you never really say anything." He acted like he hadn't heard me.

"There was a story once. You see code names, hear stories, put little bits of information together. It is so difficult..."

"The story. What is it?"

"Someone in External Affairs. Something about blackmail." He looked sadder than ever.

Blackmail. I liked that.

He continued, "But maybe it wasn't blackmail at all." What was he going on about? "Let me recall...it seems to me another interpretation of the story could be that it was supposed to look like blackmail." He stared at me. I had no idea what he was talking about.

He went on, "Soviets are very patient. Five years, ten years, a generation, it is all the same. After so many years, who knows what the truth is anymore?" He looked at me plaintively. "You will not believe me, I know. But the Russians have friends everywhere, in the government, in External, in the Mounties..."

He was right. I didn't really believe him.

Suddenly, he killed his drink and stood up. "I hope I have been of help, Mr. Smith," he growled, in his thick accent. "I must leave now."

"Hey, wait a minute!" I leapt up and grabbed his sleeve.

Very slowly, he took my hand off. "I am sure that your suspicions are well-founded. The Soviets are everywhere. Do not give up. Follow the trail to the end." He turned on his heel and hurried off. "Do not follow me." In a second, he was gone.

What suspicions? What trail? I paid the bill, thinking it was outrageously expensive. I hoped Ed hadn't finished the bottle of whiskey upstairs.

I had the sinking feeling I was paying for this trip out of my own pocket.

For three hours that night, as we nursed the bottle of whiskey and listened to the radio playing softly, Ed was apologetic about the failure of the meeting. I shrugged him off morosely, but he continued his apologies the next morning and all through the train ride back to Ottawa. "At least you can concentrate on other things, now."

I only half-listened. I was trying to put some sort of order into the things I knew and the things I needed to know. That didn't cheer me up. I felt the Russians were one key to everything, and they weren't going to talk. And Mrs. Robinson was another key, but I suspected she wasn't even aware of what she knew. It was enough to make a poor man's head burst.

We pulled into the station around noon. I bade farewell to Ed, and trudged in the noon heat towards the station.

As I passed Ogilvy's department store on Rideau Street, the heat and the discouragement overcame me, and I made a decision to forget about going to work until Monday morning. It hadn't been a long time since we got Saturday afternoons off and were working only a five-and-a-half day week, instead of six days a week. The extra half-day seemed a luxury unimaginable only a few years ago, and I intended taking advantage. That decision was a mistake.

CHAPTER 11

I grabbed a New Edinburgh streetcar deciding to forget about dropping my club-bag at home, and headed for Eastview to visit my brother and his family. I figured he'd be about ready to quit work about now. If he had any work today.

Ken's wife, Rita, noticed the club-bag. "Moving in, Pen?" I always liked Rita. She wasn't what you'd call pretty, but she was attractive enough even as she gained weight year by year with rotund regularity. The kids whooped and hollered, more from anticipation of the quarters Uncle Pen would give them than from any feeling of family love. I passed over the required quarters. Rita complained about bribery, but more for form than through true disagreement.

Ken was repairing the room of the summer kitchen out back. He was glad for a break. He suggested a couple of quick ones before supper, so we walked over to the Claude Hotel on Beechwood. We ordered a few drafts and drank them eagerly as ammunition against the heat.

Ken admitted business was real slow, but hoped it'd pick up by the fall. One more time, for the twentieth time at least, I suggested he quit construction and come into business with me. I had an idea for a small business when I retired, but I wanted to start it now, so it would be a going concern when I was ready to work at it. In the meantime, Ken could run it.

"Ken, I've checked it out. This is a perfect town. Look, there's all the embassies, and government departments, and banks and insurance companies and head offices of businesses. A small security company could make a lot of money. And I know every policeman in town, we could get them to work in their off-hours and they'd provide an image of toughness and respectability nobody else could match. It's a natural. I'll provide the capital, pay you a small salary and a percentage of profits. We both could become rich and fat and lazy with this." I sighed. I wasn't used to saying so many words in a row.

Ken remained unconvinced. He had a thousand reasons why it wouldn't work, based mainly on his own failure with the construction firm. I guess he had two difficulties really. One was admitting that most of the problems with his own business were of his own making. The other was taking a back seat to his big brother. We had a sibling rivalry going back for decades.

When we were in our twenties, we had come the closest to friendship. The Duggan brothers were well-known in the bars and clubs of Ottawa and Hull and Aylmer and Gatineau as hell-raisers and fist-throwers of great repute. Usually, it was Ken who started some trouble or other. But when the fists started flying, it was brother Pen who had to join in. Now, it was Ken who remembered those times with a perverse fondness.

"Remember the time we got beat up and thrown out of the Gatineau Club, and we had no money left and we had to walk all the way back to Papineau?"

"Yeah, and Mom was already up and making breakfast when we walked in."

"And she threw the frying pan at you for getting your little brother into trouble. And wouldn't talk to you for the whole weekend."

"And all the time it was you who started the trouble over that ex-girlfriend of yours."

"What was her name? Suzanne Lemieux. One of the Lemieuxs, remember they lived over on St. Andrew Street? Her brother ended up as inspector on the O.E.R. Started driving a streetcar about twenty years ago. I saw him the other day doin' time checks over at Bank and Somerset. He's put on a lot of weight. Pretended he didn't remember me when I talked to him."

"Yeah, he stole them blind for years as an operator, then they go and promote him. You figure it out."

"I was nuts over her, but she was always a stuck-up. Her whole family put on airs. I think their father had a job all through the Depression workin' for the city or something."

"He was in maintenance, as I remember. A glorified handyman."

"Yeah, but you didn't give up any jobs in them days, no matter how bad."

"Still don't, as far as I can see."

"No they don't. And you want me to give up on construction. It might not be much, but it's all I got." I had said the wrong thing.

"Okay, forget it, forget it. Catch the waiter, and we'll get one for the road."

"The only reason I got going was because she was out with that dumb prick from the Glebe, Daniel what's-his-name." Ken wasn't letting his reminiscences be interrupted. "Never could stand him. Remember? He useta play hockey for the Senators, the last season before they went under. Probably was his fault they hadda fold. He useta give me a hard time every chance he could. Had no business going out with a Lowertown girl." Ken had a fiercely-developed sense of territory. On the other hand, lots of people used to give him a hard time. It was his nature.

"Rita will be waiting. We should get going." We got up and left. When we got home, the house seemed abnormally quiet.

Ken noticed it first. "Where's Charlie and Danny?"

"They're over at the Jackson's. They got a television set." She aimed the last statement at me with a kind of sneer, but one with more than a tinge of envy. It would be a long time before she and Ken could afford a television.

I offered to go get the kids for supper. I wasn't above taking a look at this television myself. I had only seen one a couple of times, for a few Friday night prizefights with some of the lads from the station.

The kids screamed. "Please, please, can't we wait till it's over? Please, please, Uncle Pen!" I wasn't against waiting for the end of the program, as long as I could watch with them. Mr. Jackson extended the invitation, so I sat down with the dozen or so kids flopped on the living room floor in front of the set.

Hopalong Cassidy was on. He had hopped along a bit too late for me to have enjoyed as a kid. My cowboys were Tom Mix and Wild Bill Anderson and Hoot Gibson. I must admit I was as enthralled with Hopalong as the kids were.

After Hoppy had won the final shoot-out and said goodbye to the pretty girl rancher and her father, I gathered up the kids and thanked the Jacksons. We almost made it to the door before the next program came on. When the boys saw it was Wild Bill Hickock, they put up a new fuss. I had to invoke stern discipline to get them out the door, kicking and screaming all the while.

"I'll tell your Dad, and he won't let you go over any more." That shut them up. Boy, I would have been a good father.

Rita had a pot of corn on the cob boiling on the stove when we returned. We sat down to an evening meal of corn, tomato and cucumber sandwiches and balogna slices. It was delicious.

After supper, the adults went for a walk around the block. The heat of the day was lingering, but we were in no hurry. We chatted with neighbours, looked into store windows, checked out the movies at the Linden and decided not to go inside.

Ken and Rita waited on the streetcar stop with me until one came along. I jumped on. As the trolley pulled away, I could hear Rita yelling, "You forgot your club-bag, Pen. Come back to visit sometime and pick it up."

Back home, I indulged in a much-needed housecleaning. I bundled clothes for the laundry. I swept cobwebs. I washed dishes. I dusted furniture. I was just touching on the surface, but that was enough for me. The house smelled old and musty. There wasn't much I could do about that. It was old and musty. I was old and musty. I remembered a line in a mystery story I read one time in *Black Mask* magazine. I felt just like that guy. I felt tired and old and not much use to anybody.

During the night it rained. It didn't disturb me, I was sleeping the sleep of the dead or the innocent or something. Around five in the morning, I stood on the front porch, feeling the wetness in the air. I felt a lot better. Eight hours sleep does that to you sometimes.

While I was showering and making a bit of breakfast, I tried whistling a bit of "Glow-worm". The Mills Brothers did a better job. As bacon fried, I tried humming a few bars of "Wish You Were Here". Eddie Fisher did a better job. I had the right feeling to be a jazz musician. I liked smoky clubs at three in the morning. I liked the sweet sound of a clarinet played by somebody like Artie Shaw or Buster Bailey. I could follow every beat of Gene Krupa's drumming in my head. Billie Holiday's voice cut through my heart like a knife. The only thing missing was a bit of talent. I guess we can't all be musicians. Someone's got to be a policeman. Somebody's got to push people around, make sure they act like civilized human beings. Somebody's got to keep people from acting like the crazed animals they really are. All in all, I'd rather play trombone in Harry James's band.

For a change, I went to the eight o'clock mass. They were short an usher, so I took a collection plate around to help out. There were only about forty or fifty people there, all spread out throughout the church. Damn. Why didn't they all sit together, instead of making me plod from pew to pew? Even in church, people keep their distance from one another. I guess they really don't hear any of the sermons. I tried to use my bulk and a scowl on my face to browbeat people into giving up an extra nickel or a dime. It didn't seem to work. The take was lousy. You'd think the Depression was still on. Well, in Lowertown maybe it still was.

After the service was over, I stayed in my seat. I tried to think a little. Maybe you could call it praying. I couldn't seem to make any kind of prayerful sounds. I sure didn't feel like making a joyful noise unto the Lord. Sitting there didn't help. To hell with it. I left by the side door.

On my way home, I took the shortcut across Angel Square. A bunch of kids were playing a pick-up softball game. I walked over.

"Hey, kid, give me a swing, will you?" I held out my hand for the bat. The kid gave it to me.

The pitcher yelled, "No way, Mister! You gotta start in field and work your way up to batter."

I scowled my fiercest look. "Whatsa matter, kid, afraid of an old man?"

"Afraid? Naw, you couldn't hit one of my pitches anyway."
All the kids laughed. I had them right where I wanted now.

I loosened my tie, took off my jacket. I spit on my hands and
took a few practice swings through the air. "C'mon, kid, gimme
your best." I felt great.

I didn't feel as great when I took a cut at the first pitch. I was
far too slow. The ball was already in the catcher's mitt when I
finished my swing. All the kids laughed. The pitcher exaggerated
his mirth, rolling on the ground in glee.

The second pitch was high and outside. I looked it over,
decided to pass it up. The catcher called it a ball. At least he was
honest.

The pitcher decided to stay with his fastball. Maybe it was the
only pitch he had. He let loose another, high and outside. This
time I was ready. I took a hefty swing. The ball soared lazily into
the air, over the head of the pitcher, over the head of the centre
fielder, who watched it fly over his head, then turned and
walked to pick it up. It wasn't for real, so he wasn't going to run.
The pitcher scowled, kicking his toe into the dirt.

I waited until he looked up, handed the bat to the catcher and
smiled at the pitcher. "Better practise, kid. The Dodgers'll never
take a one-pitch wonder like you."

He moved aggressively towards the plate. "Aw, who'd wanna
play for Brooklyn anyway? They stink!"

That hurt. I tried a parting shot, hoping for a smile. "That's
okay, kid, so do you." No smile.

I put on my jacket. The catcher looked at me a long moment.
"Ain't you the cop lives over on Papineau?"

"That's right, kid." I smiled broadly, doing my best for
community relations.

"We hate cops."

So much for community relations. I walked closer, looking
directly into his soft ten-year-old eyes. "That's all right, kid. The
feeling is mutual."

The elation I had felt playing ball had suddenly deflated.
They weren't bad kids, but chances were I'd meet them again in
a couple of years, when they were arrested for assault or petty
theft. Instead of feeling like Joe Dimaggio, I felt like an abusive

father. I really didn't hate kids, I didn't know how to act around them. Not enough practice, I guess. I walked away feeling glum.

The heat of the day was just starting to burn. I sat on the front porch, watching the people go by. It was a bit past nine. A couple of kids, about seven or eight, trudged down the middle of the street carrying fishing poles and a can of worms each, dressed only in bathing trunks.

"*Où allez-vous?*" I shouted, trying out my French. In Lower-town, if you couldn't speak French, you missed half of what was going on. When I was a kid about their age, if I wasn't in the house or in school, I spoke French. All the other kids on Papineau Street were French, so if I wanted to play with them I had to learn their language. It isn't in the Irish nature to learn another language, but I was a little kid, what did I know? Besides, it came in handy later, when I went courting. It didn't hurt me during the war, either.

They stepped onto the sidewalk, looking at me gravely from behind serious, clear eyes. "Flat Rock, *Monsieur.*"

"*Bonne chance.*" I waved them on their way. They moved back into the middle of the street. My mother would have yelled to them that streets were for horses and sidewalks were for walking, but I didn't bother.

I envied them their Sunday fishing. I watched them turn the corner onto Cobourg, and in my mind I could trace their exact route, for I had walked it myself a thousand times when I was a kid. Over a couple of blocks, down St. Patrick walking on the streetcar rails, over the bridge, turn left, follow the well-worn footpath to the beach. They'd probably stop for a half-hour on the bridge and try their luck there first. They'd stop again half-way to Flat Rock for a second try. After awhile, they'd be hot and sticky, so they'd trudge the rest of the way to join the Sunday swimming crowd at Flat Rock.

They could have gone the opposite way along the river, ending up at Dutchy's, down in Sandy Hill. But that was a different gang of kids down there, and they might get beat up.

Now that I recall, there were a hundred spots on either the Ottawa or Rideau Rivers where a kid could go swimming or fishing when I was a kid. I wouldn't guess there's more than two or three now, and those closed down most of the time because of pollution. Hell, even if you could catch some fish today, you wouldn't dare eat them. But they say we have a higher standard of living today. I guess they're right, I don't know.

So that's how a lazy Sunday went by.

For supper, I made up a mess of Champ. My mother used to make Champ, mostly on Fridays when you weren't supposed to eat meat, and her mother before her, and her mother, back unto the time when Irish people hid in hedgerows from the English bullets and clubs before they had saved up a few shillings to pay for passage to America.

What you do first is boil up a bunch of potatoes. My mother always said the correct number was nine. Then you drain and mash them. Then you add a bunch of onions, all chopped up. If you want to get fancy, you can add chives or parsley or whatever you have that doesn't cost any money. Then you season with a lot of salt and pepper and beat it again.

Meanwhile, you heat up a plate in the oven. You make a big mound of Champ on the plate and push down a hole in the centre. Into this hole you put a huge chunk of butter.

You eat the Champ from the outside, dipping it into the butter in the centre, which is melting all the while. It is delicious.

It is also a meal to fuel the flames of revolt and terror, for who can eat such a gruel of submission without planning a revenge of the most horrible retribution in his deepest heart? Only when the last Irishman has eaten the last bowl of Champ will peace come to the land of my ancestors.

I filled myself up on Champ. For all of that, it's still a delicious meal.

After supper, I walked over to St. Brigid's and looked in on Father Scanlon. He poured the brandy liberally, and we sat in his parlour passing the time comfortably.

"So, what's new, Father?"

"Not much, Pen. Going to hold some revival meetings this week. Got a Jesuit preacher from the States coming up. They say he's a real hell-raising orator. Maybe you should drop in. You look like you could use a spiritual uplift."

"That's for true, Father, that's for true."

"Things not going well?"

"Nothing seems to work out." And I didn't even know the half of it.

"Well, keep working, Pen, and it will all turn out right." Father Scanlon was an eternal optimist. I guess he had to be, in his line of work.

"Yeah, that's what I'll do, Father." I held out my glass for a refill.

Father Scanlon paced the room nervously. "Mr. Larrimar was arrested last week."

"Yeah? Doesn't he work at Freiman's?"

"Used to. Seems he appropriated a few goods he wasn't entitled to." I knew what was coming. "Can you put in a good word for him, Pen? Maybe they could go easy on him."

"Seems to me, this isn't the first time he's been caught with someone else's property. Seems to me, I've put in a good word for him on at least three occasions. Seems to me, every time he promises this is the last time, and then within a year he's back at it again."

"He can't resist the occasion of sin. He's a weak man, Pen, susceptible to temptation."

"Yeah. He's a thief, Father, an unrepentent thief. And a thorough scoundrel."

"He's got five kids. It's a hard growing-up when your father is in and out of jail all the time. You must have some compassion."

"Father, I'm loaded with compassion. I feel sorry for the wife, I feel sorry for the five kids, but enough is enough. If the wife had laid a frying pan across his head years ago, he might have straightened out. Maybe if he had been sent to prison the first time, he might have straightened out. As it is..."

"Well, I can't argue with you about punishment for your sins, Pen, but I think maybe he's learned his lesson now."

"Father, if he's learned any lesson, it's that he can steal people blind, and his parish priest and a friendly neighbourhood policeman can keep him from going to jail for it."

"You'll see what you can do, won't you?" Father Scanlon refilled my glass.

I had to laugh. "Yes, Father, I'll see what I can do."

"Good. It's not as if those Jews at Freiman's will miss a few overcoats. They couldn't sell them in this heat anyway."

"Now, don't start, Father. The commandment isn't 'Thou shalt not steal, except from Jews,' it's plain 'Thou shalt not steal.'"

"Now, don't go quoting the bible at me, Pendrick Duggan, I know it a lot better than you. Don't forget the two thieves on the cross with our Saviour."

"I don't, Father, but they weren't innocent men, they were guilty as hell. One of them may have received forgiveness, but they both had to pay for their crimes. Don't forget, they were crucified, too."

"Ah, there you go, getting your stories all mixed up again. The lesson in that story is about repentence and forgiveness, not about crucifixion. You only take the lesson you want to take. You're about ready for a retreat, I should think, my boy." Another of Father Scanlon's favourite theories was that any problem in life could be solved by going on a retreat for a week, fasting and praying and keeping silent.

"If I had the time, Father, I'd love to go on a retreat. Maybe for the rest of my life."

"Now, don't go to extremes, my boy. A week in the country would do you good. I could set it up, you know."

"Maybe next year, Father."

"I hear you were out of town for a few days."

"Can't keep any secrets in this neighbourhood, can you, Father? Yep, I visited the fleshpots of Toronto." Father Scanlon pursed his lips disapprovingly. "Stayed in a big hotel. Even ate Chinese food."

"Heathen food." Father Scanlon shook his head violently. "Roast beef and potatoes, my son, now that's a Christian meal. It was good enough for our Lord, it's good enough for you. Broiled rats and all that, it's all right for the heathens themselves, but it's not Christian food." Father Scanlon's knowledge of our Lord's diet was equal to his knowledge of Chinese cuisine.

I laughed, and made my leave-taking. As usual, Father Scanlon had cheered me up. Sometimes, I think he said the most outrageous things just to get my blood boiling and give me a fighting attitude. It worked. I walked home with a fighting attitude.

The phone rang around nine. It was Bruno.

"What's up, Duggan?"

I brought him more or less up to date. "Why you asking?"

"Maybe I shouldn't say nothin', but I got called into the Chief's office yesterday. He was fulla questions. And they were all about you. You pullin' some fast stuff on the Chief you haven't told me about?"

"Nothing I can think of right now."

"You're always pullin' somethin', Duggan. You must be holdin' somethin' back. Why else would the Chief be askin' about you?" Bruno was a great believer in the smoke and fire theory.

"I haven't reported yet on my Toronto trip. But that's all."

"Well, maybe that's it. I sure hope the Chief's not gonna come down hard on you with both boots."

I hoped so, too.

I didn't sleep well that night. My ribs ached. I was still passing blood. Lucille invaded my dreams, laughing at me and tempting me and rejecting me and loving me and hating me.

I woke up in a sweat and leapt from the bed as if it was cursed.

I felt more tired than I had when I had gone to bed. With a dull, piercing headache, I walked to the station in the coolness of the dawn. It was not going to be the best day I had ever had.

CHAPTER 12

For a change, it was warmer in the station than it was outside. That would only last an hour or two. The radio was predicting a high of ninety-seven.

They were seated on folding chairs next to my desk. There were two of them. Plainclothes, both over six feet, both scowling with impatience. I was curious, so I walked over.

They stood together. "Detective Duggan?"

I admitted I was Detective Duggan and sat on my chair to look through my telephone messages.

They pulled out identical identification from identical wallets. I had a sense of déjà vu.

"Inspector Wallace. This is Inspector Sherman." Good Anglo-Saxon names. "Internal Affairs. We got some questions. Maybe you got some answers."

Where did these guys get their dialogue? They must watch *Dragnet* on television. I had heard of it, but had never seen it. I had also heard of Internal Affairs, and their role was investigation of policemen who had slipped from the paths of righteousness, taken bribes, assaulted citizens, that sort of thing. I guessed that the Russians had made an assault complaint against me. Wrong guess.

"Sure, gentlemen, what can I do for you? Whatever it is, I'm innocent as a newborn lamb." I gave them my best innocent look.

"Wipe that smile off your face, Duggan. We're not here to play games." If they were going to play the nice guy-mean guy game, Wallace was going to be the mean one. "Let's go."

I stood up. "Where we going?"

"Interrogation room. This way." I knew the way without their directions.

Sherman slammed the door. Wallace found a pack of Black Cat cigarettes in his pocket, lit one, and threw the pack on the table. "Sit down, Duggan."

"Sure, Wallace." I figured I'd push a bit, to see exactly where I stood.

Sherman leapt to the attack first. He wasn't playing the nice guy at all. "It's 'Sir' to you, Duggan. Don't forget it."

"Yes, Sir!" I put as much sarcasm into it as I could.

"Shut your fuckin' mouth, Duggan!" Wallace's scream reached Parliament Hill, I'm sure. It was meant to.

"Answer the questions, and don't talk unless you've got an answer." Sherman leaned close to me. His breath stank. I turned my face towards Wallace.

"Trouble, always trouble. There's one rotten apple in every basket. Ain't it the truth?" Wallace was either asking me a question or else waxing poetic.

"Yessir." I was trying to be helpful.

"Who asked you?" Sherman again. "Wait for the question."

"I did."

"You did what?"

"Wait for the question. You asked, 'Ain't that the truth?' "

"I read your files, Duggan, don't think I didn't. I spent the whole weekend reading your files, and a disgusting story it is." Wallace was getting worked up. "Full of reprimands, suspensions, demotions. Cops like you make me sick. When you pin on a badge, you're in a position of public trust. When you violate that trust, it affects each and every one of your fellow officers. It makes me sick." I was getting more and more confused, wondering what made him so sick.

"May I ask what exactly your problem is?"

"I told you to shut the fuck up unless we ask you a question." Sherman looked like he was going to hit me. I looked him in the eye, telling him silently that that would be a big mistake. He backed away. "We don't got no problem. You're the one with the problem."

Wallace took up the theme. "When you're booted off the force, you forfeit your pension. Twenty-three years down the drain, Duggan, twenty-three years. Think about that when you answer."

I broke an abstention of twelve years when I reached over and took one of Wallace's Black Cats. It tasted every bit as good as I remembered. I was both confused and scared. Guys like Wallace and Sherman were heavyweights. They only moved to the interrogation stage when all the evidence was already in. I was about to be hanged, and I hadn't the slightest clue what for.

I waited for one of them to drop the first clue.

Wallace moved to the attack first. "Betcha wish you had a drink now, don't you, Duggan?" He turned to address Sherman. "Fuckin' alcoholics. The force is riddled with them. Take away their bottle and they couldn't solve their way out of a traffic jam." He butted his cigarette furiously with his boot.

They didn't ordinarily bring in Internal Affairs to discuss an officer's drinking problems. If they did, I'm sure the poor lads would have no time left for any other investigations.

"No, sir." I tried to look humble.

"No, sir, what?"

"I never take a drink before noon." I lied, but I didn't think they'd hold it against me. "Well, maybe eleven, if it's a special occasion."

"This is a special occasion, Duggan. Special for us, that is. Because today we get to hang you out to dry." Wallace smiled as he spoke softly. I dragged on my cigarette. I knew they'd get to the point sooner or later.

Sherman opened the file he had in his hand. Wallace took out a pen and notebook. Here it comes.

"Tell us all about her, Duggan."

"All about who...sir?"

"Who do you think, Duggan? Your wife, of course."

For the first and only time in my life, I almost fainted. After eight years, it had finally come.

"My wife's dead, sir."

Wallace threw his notebook on the table, bunched his fists furiously. He loomed over me, a murderous look in his eyes. "Of course she's dead, you miserable son of a bitch! What we want to know is, why did you kill her?"

I followed Wallace's example and butted my cigarette on the floor. "Nobody killed her. She committed suicide." I felt like the past eight years had been only an interlude between interrogations.

Sherman pretended to read from the file. "Suicide, eh? You know there's no statute of limitations on murder, don't you Duggan?"

"Yessir, I know."

"You've had a good long run, but it's over now. You may as well confess, it'll make you feel better. You can't go through life with the fear of discovery hanging over your head. It'll drive you crazy. We found you out, and it'll go a lot easier on you if you just make a clean breast of it." For the first time, Wallace smiled. He held his pencil on his notepad, waiting. I let him wait.

It's funny that they use the same interrogation techniques on fellow officers as they do on the general public. You'd think that policemen, knowing all the textbook techniques, would be less susceptible to them. Maybe they're so psychologically correct, they work on you whether you know the theory or not. I certainly felt like confessing. I resisted the urge.

"You're both crazy. Sirs."

Sherman smiled this time. "We'll see, Duggan, we'll see. Okay, let's go through it step by step, just like it happened eight years ago. Only this time, don't leave out anything, and fill in all the details on how you killed her."

"I can't do that. I didn't kill her. I was in Montreal at the time. Attending a law enforcement conference."

"That's your alibi, Duggan. Think a good cop could break that alibi?"

I admit sometimes I let my tongue get the best of me. I smiled as I said it. "A good cop might. You guys can't."

That was when they hit me the first time. Wallace came flying across the desk and punched me in the nose. Growling, I stood up, raising my fists. My mistake.

Sherman came behind me and grabbed me in a bear hug,

pinning my arms. Wallace hit me solidly in the ribs with a left, then a right, as I struggled to break free. Then he gave me a rabbit punch to the neck as I bent over to protect myself. Sherman rammed me against the wall then onto the floor. They both put their boots to my ribs. They had read my file all right, including the part about my night in Voscovitch's apartment.

They pulled me up and threw me into a chair. Wallace hit me a few dozen times with the back of his hands, first the left, then the right. Then the left. And the right. It seemed to go on and on. I was spitting blood, yelling and crying, all at the same time.

All that swinging seemed to tire Wallace out. With a heave, he threw himself back. Sherman had been leaning against the wall all the while, so I thought he'd take his turn. Instead, they both walked out without a word, leaving me to bleed all over the table and the floor. I didn't move for the ten minutes they were gone.

Sherman came in with a wet towel. He threw it against my face. "Here, clean yourself up. You look a mess. God, you disgust me!" He stood over me as I wiped my face off.

Wallace came back in. He lit himself a cigarette, watching me silently. Then he lit another Black Cat and placed it between my lips. It tasted horrible. I sucked hungrily on it anyway.

They had established their credentials. Wallace smiled lazily. Sherman took the towel away and left the room.

"You're a fool, Duggan. You think you're going to sweat this investigation and walk right back to your desk. Why, I'll just bet you're thinking about revenge against me and Sherman right now. Even as we speak, I bet you're thinking up some fantasy about getting each of us in an alley one night and cutting our balls off. Ain't that right, Duggan?

"Well, you can forget your fuckin' fantasies. Because this is real life, and you're never gonna get no revenge. So don't even think it.

"And you want to know why? Because you're finished in the force as of right now. Whether you confess or not. We've got you dead to rights. Even if we can't ever convict you, we know you killed your wife, Duggan. And we can't let a killer stay on the force now, can we?"

I wondered if that was a question I should answer. I took a chance. My voice sounded very far away. I spit more blood.

"No."

"I'm glad you agree. Mind you, a confession would tie things up neatly. Want to confess now?"

"No."

"I didn't think so." Sherman came back into the room. Wallace continued. "The reason you don't want to confess is because you don't know all the evidence we got against you. Ain't I right, Inspector Sherman?"

Sherman nodded his agreement. "So right, Inspector Wallace."

I raised my head. It was painful, but somehow I was in a somewhat cooperative mood.

"What evidence?"

"He wants to know what evidence, Inspector Sherman. Why don't you tell him what evidence."

"We got your army records, Duggan. Your fuckin' army records."

"And if we had of read your fuckin' army records when you came back after the war, we wouldn't have let you back on the force again, Duggan. If we hadda read your army records, we would have known eight years ago that you killed your wife. Ain't that the truth, Inspector Sherman?"

"That's the truth."

My army records. I tried to clear my head, tried to think. They weren't about to let me.

"So, Duggan, let's go back eight years. You hated your wife, didn't you, Duggan? You hated her 'cause she was runnin' around on you when you were overseas."

"I didn't hate her."

"'Course you did. It's natural. We don't blame you, we just want you to admit it."

It was a long day. They kept after me, coming at Lucille's death from every possible angle, never giving me a chance to think, never giving me a chance to explain. After awhile, I couldn't remember what I had said before. I wanted another cigarette, I wanted a rest. I wanted them to stop asking questions.

Sometime during the afternoon, they hit me some more. They left my face alone, concentrating on my ribs and my groin. That's when I stopped answering their questions. It didn't seem to surprise them. They continued asking questions for another two hours. Then they closed their notebook and file and went away. I hoped they'd stay away for a long time.

When they came back, the Chief was with them. He ignored all evidence of violence. He looked grim.

"Duggan, Duggan, Duggan." The Chief was given to repetition. "What are we going to do with you, Duggan?"

I didn't think the question required an answer.

"I must admit, you had me fooled all these years, Duggan." The Chief paced the floor, his hands clasped behind his back. "Never for a minute did I think you'd betray my trust in you. I guess you had us all fooled." The Chief sighed, no doubt comforted by the thought that he was not the only one I had fooled so easily. "You know what gave you away, Duggan?" I knew. My army records. The army records they had spent the whole weekend going through. "Your army records. They established a method of operation, a pattern of crime."

"Of course, during the war, it wasn't a crime at all, Duggan. You learned your lessons, and put them into operation in the field. During wartime, that is to be commended. But you put them into operation during peacetime, didn't you, Duggan?

"And we would never had known unless we got a peek into your army records, that your specialty in wartime underground operations was disposing of enemy agents and making it look like suicide. It says you were successful on at least four occasions. They weren't sure about another three people, whether they were officially accepted as suicides or not.

"You know, when Lucille died, I had the feeling something was wrong, but I just couldn't put my finger on it." The Chief was lying now, trying to rewrite history. "There's a fair number of policemen commit suicide, I know that. But not their wives. The wives live to collect half-pensions in their old age. That's what was funny about Lucille's death.

"Inspectors Wallace and Sherman tell me that you refuse to confess even though they've given you ample opportunity."

If it didn't hurt so much, I would have smiled. "Nevertheless, I believe that with your wartime record and with circumstantial evidence, we could make a case stick against you. I know you were supposed to be at a conference in Montreal, but you could have come back to Ottawa in only two hours, killed your wife, and returned to your bed no one the wiser.

"Yessir, I think we have a case here."

I had finally had enough. Taking hold of the table, I pulled myself to my feet. I stood there weaving, feeling like I would fall over any second.

"There's only one thing wrong." I coughed up some more blood. The Chief turned his head away. "It's not true." Wallace and Sherman and the Chief all looked at each other with disbelief. I was shattering their little plot to convict Duggan without a trial.

"Not only is it not true, but you wouldn't even know where to find witnesses from eight years ago. I admit I did some shabby things when I was overseas. But I was ordered to do them. It doesn't follow that I continued after the war." I broke down into a coughing spell. I steadied myself against the table.

"You can't possibly have a case against me, because Lucille committed suicide. The investigating officers said so. The coroner said so. The crown prosecutor said so. The attorney general's office said so. And Internal Affairs said so. Eight years ago. And in them days, Internal had a crack bunch of investigators. Not like Donald and Mickey here." Wallace and Sherman didn't like that crack. I didn't care anymore.

The Chief pursed his lips and furrowed his brow thoughtfully. "Detective Duggan, as of midnight Thursday, you have been on suspension. Without pay. At this stage of our investigations, we will not jail you." He made it sound like the biggest favour he could offer. "You will return to the station at eight a.m. tomorrow morning for further interrogation. After that, we will decide whether to prefer charges or not."

I let go of the desk, and stumbled over to stand in front of the Chief.

"No."

The three exchanged glances.

"No?"

"No. I didn't kill Lucille. You have no chance of proving I did. I'm not going through another investigation. Decide what you want. I'm through answering questions. It's long ago and far away, Lucille's suicide. Put me in jail or let me go home."

Wallace and Sherman and the Chief retreated to a far corner of the room to talk things over. I couldn't hear what they were saying. I took hold of the edge of the desk again. It looked like the Chief was arguing against the other two, but it might have been a show-and-tell for my benefit. The Chief returned to stand in front of me.

"Duggan, you'll go home now. You will return here tomorrow at eight a.m. At that time, we shall decide what steps will be taken. You may go now."

"Just one more thing." Using the table to steady myself, I made my way slowly to Wallace. I hit him with all my strength. I had hardly any left. He didn't even flinch. I fell to the floor. The Chief looked disgusted.

"Take him home."

Wallace and Sherman each took an armpit and pulled me to my feet. The bastards dragged me through the station house so everyone could see I was under investigation by Internal Affairs. I've no doubt it struck fear into a few hearts.

They threw me into the back of an unmarked squad car and drove me home. Between them, they got me onto the verandah. Sherman found my doorkey, opened the door and pushed me inside. I fell onto the hallway linoleum.

"So long, tough guy." I wasn't sure who said that.

"So long, ex-Detective." That was the other one.

I put my head down on the cool linoleum and slept.

It was sometime in the midnight hour when I woke. I didn't remember where I was. I looked around groggily, until I recognized the flowered wallpaper on the wall. For some reason, lying there in the blood and the pain, I distinctly remembered the summer afternoon day thirty years before when I helped my mother put up that wallpaper. Incongruously, I made a mental note to re-paper the hallway.

After a long moment lying there, I tried to stand. I couldn't seem to make my legs hold me up. I crawled into the living room area, and towards the stairs. I used the bannister to rise to my feet, but after three steps I lowered myself and crawled the rest of the way upstairs.

I crawled into the bathroom and turned the bath on. While it filled, I took off my clothes. I seemed to have blood running all over my body. Hooking one leg over the lip of the tub, I splashed into it. I couldn't seem to find the strength to sit up to turn off the taps, so I used my foot. There was a little drip that I couldn't stop.

I lay there, not thinking about anything, just letting the warmth of the water soothe my aches. I watched, fascinated, as the water slowly turned a pinkish red.

After what seemed like several hours, I felt good enough to hook my elbows over the side of the tub and pull myself to a sitting position. I sat there, letting the pink water cool around me.

Eventually, my brain started functioning again. I thought about the Chief and Wallace and Sherman. I thought about Mrs. Robinson. I thought about Igor Gouzenko and Sergeant Carson and Ed Lukowicz. But mostly I thought about Lucille.

I hadn't meant to cause Lucille's death, of course.

It was a stupid plan I had, a plan to catch her in the middle of one of her tawdry affairs, confront her with the evidence and arrange some sort of separation. The plan went screwy, and that's the plain truth of it.

When I returned from overseas, the evidence of Lucille's faithlessness became more and more apparent as time went by. I realized that both my mother and my brother had tried to hint about it in their letters to me. In those days, you didn't talk about such things openly. I became fairly sure, but not positive, that Lucille was committing adultery every chance she had. The irony was that the number of possible affairs, when I added them up in my mind, were so astronomical as to appear impossible.

What could have happened to turn such passionate lovers into such bitter enemies? I guess it was mainly my fault. Having won Lucille, I then proceeded to ignore her, first as a policeman and then as a soldier. It never occurred to me to take her for anything other than granted. Those were different days back then. A husband did whatever he wanted to do. It never occurred to me that a wife would take whatever revenge she could.

In my stupidity, I thought that the fact that I never cheated on Lucille would make up for all my other mistakes. I was wrong.

I laid my plans carefully. I made sure Lucille knew I was spending a weekend at a police conference in Montreal. Late on the Saturday night, I returned to Ottawa, hid the car a few blocks from the apartment we had rented on Guigues Street, and stationed myself in a doorway across the street.

Around two in the morning, the man came from our apartment, got into a blue Ford coupe and drove away. I made a note of his licence number and went into the apartment building.

I slammed the door to our apartment.

"Pen? Is that you Pen?"

I said nothing, prowling the apartment, sniffing the air. I could smell whiskey, perfume and sweat.

Lucille came into the living room holding her nightgown tightly around her. She was half-drunk.

"Pen? What the hell are you doing home?"

"Thought I'd surprise you. Come home for a little loving."

"I don't believe you."

"But I see you've already had your loving for the night."

"Don't be silly."

I took the slip of paper from my pocket. Talked like a policeman. "About six foot, brown hair, mustache, no hat, dark pants, tan raincoat, drives a blue Ford Coupe, licence EM 4224. Last seen leaving the domicile of Pendrick Duggan and his loving wife Lucille."

Lucille took a cigarette, lit it, waved the smoke away from her face. She looked tired.

"You're crazy!"

"Don't call me crazy. I'm not crazy. Well, maybe I am, but it's because of jealousy."

She got up and began pacing the floor. I don't know exactly what I expected. Contrition, maybe. Promises for the future. Something like that. Maybe it was because she had been drinking, but she was having none of it.

"Do you know how long you were overseas? Six goddamn years. You know how old I was when you left? Twenty-four. Did you really expect me to spend the best part of my twenties sitting in a room waiting for you?"

It's funny, German propaganda during the war was based on the idea that we soldiers should quit and go home because all our wives and girlfriends were fooling around on us. The padrés and the morale officers spent a lot of time trying to counter this effective propaganda. I guess I knew that a lot of women would be lonely back home and there would be a fair amount of adultery. But not my Lucille.

"And I suppose you're going to tell me you didn't have any fun while you were gone?" No, I wasn't going to tell her that. But we were home now. The war was over.

I called her a lot of foul names. Then she called me a lot of foul names. What had once been love spilled into hatred.

That's when I hit her. I slapped her across the head, sending her sprawling onto the floor. I admit my plan was to beat her black and blue before I left. I hit people too much, I know that.

The Luger I had brought back from the war as a souvenir was in a drawer in the bedroom. She broke free and came back aiming it at me. I wasn't worried. She had no idea how to remove the safety catch. She probably didn't even know there was one.

Calmly, I walked over to her, smiling, daring her in my silence to shoot. Her eyes were wide with excitement and fear.

"Don't come any closer!" She stepped back in indecision. "Come any closer and I'll kill myself." As if in a comic opera, she turned the pistol on herself, aiming it at her temple.

I smiled, in my arrogance daring her to kill herself. I reached over to her.

"Here. Move this piece of metal over. If you don't, the gun will never fire." I knew she'd never remove the safety catch.

She moved the safety catch.

Whatever thoughts I might have had, whatever movement I might have made, whatever arguments I might have used were lost in the roar of gunfire which tore off the top of her head.

I didn't cry. I had a sudden incongruous thought that I had never known that she hated me so much as to kill herself.

As a policeman, I knew I was an innocent man. Why, then, did I not call to report her suicide? I had done nothing but teach her how to take her life. Maybe I had been doing that already for ten years.

Instead, I turned and walked out of the apartment, wiping my fingerprints from the doorknob. I didn't bend over and hold her in my arms. I didn't say a prayer. I drove back to my police conference in Montreal.

Suicide was an obvious verdict. All the nosy neighbours knew about the men who came by when I was on duty. Most made a display of sympathy, but secretly held the cuckolded husband in contempt.

The investigating officers tried to keep the truth about all the men from me, but it had to come out in the end. Everybody walked softly around me. They took my heavy silence for grief.

None of Lucille's friends came to her funeral. The next day, I sold the car, and I've never driven since.

I was never able to make a true confession and receive absolution for my sin. One Sunday morning, I confessed all my wartime sins. I confessed to killing eight people. Only seven of them had actually died in the war. Lucille was the eighth, but the priest didn't know that. He gave me absolution, but I know it doesn't really count.

After Lucille died, I refused to cry. Now, in the pink water of my bathtub, I cried.

Even as I cried, though, I knew I wasn't going to let the Chief and Wallace and Sherman hand me over to the hangman.

I'll go to my grave with Lucille's death condemning my soul.

CHAPTER 13

I don't remember how I got into bed, but I awoke in the morning lying naked on blood-stiffened sheets. Slowly, carefully, I rose and dressed. Coming downstairs was the hardest part. I used the bannister to steady myself.

Out on the street, a squad car and a uniformed constable waited for me. I sat in the back seat.

"Home, Jeeves." The constable didn't smile. He put the car into gear, glanced at me through the rear-view mirror and drove jerkily to the corner. With increasing smoothness and speed, we wound our way towards the station.

Nobody greeted me when I walked in. People turned their heads away when I approached or else walked quickly away in the opposite direction. A real bunch of swell guys.

In the Chief's office, Wallace and Sherman were seated. Bruno was lounging against the wall. He gave a small wave of the hand and a half-smile. Maybe I hadn't been entirely abandoned after all.

The Chief scurried in, took his seat. He didn't say anything for a long while.

"Duggan, let me outline the situation for you." He tapped his folded hands on his forehead, his elbows on the desk. "We have been forced, by new information, to re-open the case of your wife's death. While the investigation unfolds, you will remain on suspension." Bruno came off the wall, rubbing his hands on his trousers. "Detective Brunowski will assume responsibility for your caseload." He glared at me, as if daring me to object. I said nothing. Wallace and Sherman exchanged glances.

The Chief continued. "I'd advise you to retain legal counsel." He was speaking very carefully and formally, as if we hadn't known each other for eighteen years. "While you are under suspension, you will not – I repeat, will not – have any contact with any of the persons involved in any of your former cases." I was in the past tense already.

He turned to Brunowski. "Detective Brunowski, Mister Duggan was investigating two deaths in this city. Both of those investigations are properly within the jurisdiction of the RCM Police. You will turn those cases over to Superintendent Francis. Today." Bruno said nothing. He gave the Chief a sort of mock salute. "Duggan, you will report to this office each morning at eight a.m. You will make yourself available for interrogation at all times. You will not leave the city. Any questions?"

I had a million questions, but I didn't ask any of them.

"No."

"That will be all for now." He waved us all out of the office. Wallace smirked. Sherman smirked. Bruno put his arm around my shoulder. It was a tiny gesture of solidarity, but it made me feel like crying. He grinned.

"I don't believe a word of it, Duggan. I'll keep my ear to the ground and let you know what I hear." He walked off with a wave of his hand. Wallace and Sherman had disappeared. Probably to find new evidence against me. Or to manufacture some.

When I stepped out onto the street, the two guys from the American Embassy were waiting beside their black Chev.

"Hop in, Duggan." The younger of the two held the rear door open. I got in.

"Hear you got no official status any more, Duggan. Too bad." I was hardly listening.

"Get your guns back, fellows?" I asked quietly. That shut them up.

Ten minutes later, we pulled up in front of the embassy, with its oversize American flag, across the street from the Parliament Buildings. I turned and looked across the street. I could see Mountie Headquarters, the Senate and the Chateau Laurier. I walked past the Marine on guard at the door. He didn't salute me. I gave him a friendly wave. He didn't smile.

The ambassador greeted me in a downstairs waiting room. A picture of Dwight Eisenhower was on the wall.

"Well, well, Mr. Duggan. We meet at last."

"Yeah."

"I must say, Mr. Duggan, it is not often that a smalltown Canadian cop will dare to pit his will against that of the U.S. ambassador. There's prime ministers and cabinet members who wouldn't try it. Well, maybe Clarence Howe would, but he doesn't count. He was born in the States."

Howe was the minister of trade and commerce, and held a half-dozen other portfolios as well. A Boston-born bundle of energy and strength who many thought really ran the Canadian government. He had never impressed me.

"Howe's an arrogant prick. Still and all, he's a Liberal. That's something."

"Well said, Mr. Duggan, well said. I've often thought of him in those terms myself, without the consolation of his liberalism." The ambassador smiled.

I didn't. "What do you want from me?"

"I must say, events seemed to have overtaken us, what with your being on suspension from the police force. Perhaps there is nothing you can do for me any more."

"Good. Maybe I can leave now."

"Not so fast." His smile had disappeared. "Sit down, Mr. Duggan." He opened a file and glanced at it. "What's the story about this Russian being killed?"

"I wish I knew. I haven't had time to find out anything. I'm off the case now. It's going to the Mounties."

"Good. Good. Always admired the Mounties. Crack law enforcement agency. Work hand in glove with the FBI. Teach them a thing or two sometimes. I like that. I admire the Mounties. The president admires them. J. Edgar does, too." He made it sound like a triumverate, with Hoover on the top. "Unlike you, the Mounties will be pleased to keep me informed of the results of their investigation."

"Good for you. Good for them." I was getting bored.

"In the army, they had a phrase to describe somebody like you, Duggan. They would say you have an attitude problem."

"My mother used to tell me that. It goes with the territory. Mind you, check my record. The number of unsolved murder cases I've investigated is zero. Maybe it's my attitude."

Fire crackled from the ambassador's eyes. His brows furrowed. He leaned back in his chair, staring at a spot behind my left shoulder.

"Somebody told me you were smart, Duggan, but you're not as smart as you think. You think I got you down here to ask you to let a murder case go unsolved. Well, maybe you're a little bit right. But only a little bit. It's a lot more complicated than you think."

"It usually is."

"I think I know why I'm having trouble talking with you. I'm not used to talking to working cops. I'm more used to other diplomats, bureaucrats, government ministers, people who know what you mean without you having to spell it out."

I laughed. It made my ribs hurt so I stopped laughing real fast. The ambassador gave me a look of concern.

"I don't usually need anyone to draw me a picture, ambassador. But if I'm going to get a proposition, I like to have the terms drawn really clear. Makes it easier to accept or reject."

"Let me try something on you, Duggan." He wasn't leaning back any more. He stared into my eyes. Probably trying his Dale Carnegie sincerity on me. "What would you say if I told you it was in the security interests of America that this Voscovitch person be found to have been killed by the Russians?"

"If it wasn't the truth, I'd tell you to go to hell."

"What would you say if I admitted she was killed by American agents, but it was in America's security interests that the killer be protected?"

"Same thing."

The ambassador smiled broadly. "There. You see why you have to be taken off the case, Duggan. You're uncooperative. You're inadvertently working for the other side. Maybe not so inadvertently. You don't like Americans too much, do you?"

"I have no stake in American security interests. It's all the same to me whether America is secure or not. It's not my country. I feel the same way about Germany or Poland or India.

Matter of fact, I'm more concerned about this city than even Canada's security. Far as I can see, it's all a game you guys play, mostly for political jockeying. I can read the papers same as everybody else."

"You've got me pegged wrong, Duggan. I'm not one of those McCarthyites you read about. Matter of fact, I'm totally opposed to his allegations and his tactics. It's my president he's attacking. My loyalty lies towards Dwight Eisenhower. It's partly a personal thing, I served under him in Europe."

That surprised me, but it didn't seem to make him any more likeable.

"The easy thing is just to tell me the truth, and let me decide how to handle the investigation."

"Now we come to the issue. You know why we can't do that, Duggan? Because we can't trust you to do the right thing. The truth of who killed Voscovitch is not nearly as important as the wider truth of stopping the spread of communism."

"Well, now, that's interesting. As an argument, it surely sounds like one your Senator McCarthy would be comfortable with."

"Well, I'm not going to spend any more time sparring verbally with you. Facts are facts. You're off the investigation. I would have tried to persuade you to give up the case, but you played the smart-alec and gave my emissaries the runaround." Emissaries. I liked that word. Very diplomatic. "Then you left town for four days. While you were away, all hell broke loose. So now it's somebody else's file."

"And you didn't have anything to do with all hell breaking loose?"

"Not a thing. Events took their course. I wouldn't have anything to do with getting a man framed on a murder charge." He smiled thinly.

"There's still something missing. I can see you sending your goons to pick me up the other day, but I don't see the reason today." He looked pained at the reference to goons. He liked to think of them as emissaries.

"I know your type, Duggan, I've met enough of them in the army. Either they end up with a chestful of medals or a bellyful of lead, 'cause they disobey orders. On suspension or not, I know you might try to cause trouble. I just wanted you here today to give you a friendly warning. When the Mounties solve your two cases, the murder charge will no doubt be dropped and you'll be back on the force. Stay out of it."

"Sounds more like my marchin' orders than a friendly warning." I rose and squared my hat on top of my head. "Well, lad, as far as I can see, this has been a waste of my time as well as yours. Far as I can see, my time'll be taken up fighting this suspension for the next while. Diplomats jumping from windows, Russian ladies dying in parks, that's small potatoes to me now. You've no worries on my account, no worries at all."

I walked towards the door. He must have pressed a hidden button, for the two emissaries were suddenly inside the door.

"Give Mr. Duggan a ride home, will you, boys." He walked out a back door.

Outside on Wellington Street, we got into the Chev. The Marine still didn't salute. As we turned onto Sussex, I leaned forward. "Let's make a wee detour, boys. Drop me off at the General Hospital instead, please. It's not far."

The driver looked at me through the rear-view mirror. "Rough interrogation?"

"Rough enough. I even learned a few new ways to hurt people. I thought I knew just about every way possible." I was exaggerating, like you always do with shop-talk.

The guy in the passenger seat twisted around, put his head over the seat. "They make you talk?"

"Didn't have anything to say."

"We could make you talk." He glanced at his buddy. They both smiled. They were bragging now. I sighed.

"I don't doubt it. If it's a serious interrogation, and you have enough time, you can make anyone talk. If you were serious about it, I'd talk soon as the door closed. In a sooner-or-later situation, I'd take sooner. It's a lot less painful."

"Your friends weren't serious."

I shrugged. "In a frame-up, you don't expect any information, you just go through the motions. Still hurts, though." We were stuck in heavy traffic. The driver cursed an idiot who made a left turn on a red light, cutting us off.

"You ever interrogate anyone with serious intent?" They sounded genuinely interested.

"Not me. But I was present for an interrogation once, during the war. I watched and learned."

"What's the story?"

"French underground. Someone was leaking information to the Gestapo. I fingered him to the group. It took them about seven hours to break him. He should have talked right away. They ended up killing him anyway, but by that time he was a sorry sight to see. He should have talked in the first hour. That was my advice to him, but he wouldn't listen. Had to prove he was a tough guy, I guess."

"Tough guys break too."

"Yeah. It's a fact of life. Felt a bit sorry for him, though. He thought he was protecting his wife and kids, who the Gestapo had arrested. Truth of the matter was, they had been killed months before."

"The guy was fighting for nothing."

"The Germans kept him on a string. When they killed the wife and kids, they kept photos, I.D.'s, clothing. When the guy demanded proof they were still alive, they fed him stuff taken off the dead bodies. Very organized people, the Germans."

They were silent, thinking about the Gestapo's methods of organization, no doubt. We arrived at the hospital.

"Mr. Duggan, I am afraid I must call the police. According to hospital records, this is the second time this week we have treated you. Two of the ribs originally cracked are now broken. Three other ones are now cracked. You may now have permanent kidney damage. Obviously, you are the victim of brutal beatings." The young doctor beamed sincerity and naivety.

"Forget it, Doctor. I am the police." I reached for my wallet, but the pain and the tight bandages made me wince. "Reach into my wallet there."

Very carefully, he opened the wallet, as if afraid of what he might find. When he saw my identification, he smiled tightly. "Sorry, Detective."

"That's all right, Doctor, thanks for worrying. See anyone else in the shape I'm in, stick to your instincts and call the police. Especially if it's a woman."

The doctor looked incredulous, like a beat-up woman was the most scandalous thing he had ever heard. I liked him, but he sure had a lot to learn about real life. A few months in the emergency department would teach him.

I skulked through the halls on my way out, hoping I wouldn't run into Sister Mary Agnes. She didn't seem to be on duty. I was glad. I didn't need another scolding.

Around midnight, the phone rang. I had been asleep since late afternoon, so I woke easily.

"Yeah?"

"Mr. Duggan?" It was a woman's voice.

"This is Duggan."

"It's Martha Robinson, Mr. Duggan." I was instantly awake.

"How do you do, Mrs. Robinson?"

"I'm in terrible trouble."

"Well, how can I help you?"

"I don't know, I'm not sure..." It sounded like she was crying.

"Please stay calm, Mrs. Robinson. First, what kind of trouble are you in?"

"They came for me..." Her crying was now wailing.

"Who came for you, Mrs. Robinson? Where did they come?"

"Two men. They broke into the apartment where I'm staying. First, they banged on the door, but before I could answer it, they broke it down." She sobbed for a moment, then cut it off with a sniffle.

"Then what?"

"I was scared. I climbed out onto the fire escape. Mr. Duggan, you've got to help me. I've never had anything like this happen before. I don't know what to do."

I tried to figure out what was happening. It sounded like a police raid to me, but that didn't make any sense. Maybe the two Americans? What about the Mounties? It couldn't be Bruno. Russians, maybe?

"What should I do, Mr. Duggan?"

"Where are you now?"

"I'm in a phone booth, outside the bus station on Albert Street."

"Did they follow you?"

"No, I don't think so...." More sniffles.

"Okay. Go into the station, find a women's rest room. Lock yourself into a cubicle. I'll get there as fast as I can. I'll knock on the door, and ask for a funny name... what about Phoebe?" Her sobs mingled with a small laugh. "Phoebe – is that all right?"

"Yes, Phoebe."

"Don't come out until you hear me ask for Phoebe. And especially don't come out if anyone asks for you by your real name." The odds against that happening were astronomical, but I wanted her mind occupied with playing a game. "You got that?"

"Yes."

"Okay. Walk, don't run, into the station. Go. I'll be there within the hour."

After she hung up, I called my brother. "Ken? Sorry to wake you. But I'm in real trouble, and I need transportation. Please help me. Pack an overnight bag, bring along my club-bag, and get your truck over to the corner of York and Chapel. Please hurry."

I'll give him credit that he asked no questions. Within twenty minutes, I was jumping into the passenger seat.

"Where we going?"

"Bus depot on Albert."

He drove silently for five minutes.

"Going to tell me what's going on?"

"My witness. Remember I was telling you about the suicide at the Chateau? The wife of the suicide victim – if that's what he was – is being chased by some thugs. I've got to hide her out for awhile."

"Why don't you just take her to the station? Or give her a police guard?" Ken wasn't stupid, not by any means.

"It's a long story." He accepted that.

I felt foolish poking my head into the women's washrooms and asking for Phoebe. She wasn't in the first one, but she came out of the second, holding a handkerchief to her eyes.

"Okay, okay." I smiled, and she put her head on my chest. It felt good. "Let's get out of here. Try not to cry, and hold onto my arm just like I'm your boyfriend or something."

She did like I asked. That felt good, too. She mumbled something about a fantasy, but I wasn't sure whose fantasy we were fulfilling, mine or hers. I didn't ask.

She clambered into the cab of the truck.

"Sorry about the mode of transportation. But this is an emergency. This is Ken. This is Mrs. Robinson. Let's move."

"Where are we going?"

"Out of town. Head west. I'll tell you where to go." First, I had to figure for myself where we would go. I had a sudden thought.

"Head for Fitzroy Harbour." Ken drove fast. Within an hour we were on the ferry, heading across to the Quebec side. We landed at Quyon. Ken laughed all the way across.

"Why is he laughing so much?" She was still holding onto my arm. I was trying to think, but having a hard time.

"It's an old story. Every St. Patrick's Day, a bunch of Irish lads from Ottawa and the rest of the Valley all go to Gavan's Hotel to celebrate. It's a real big piss-up. I don't know how the tradition got started, but it's been going on since St. Patrick booted the snakes out of Ireland, I think."

"Then, why are we going there?"

"If I was chasing someone, I'd put roadblocks on all the bridges leading out of Ottawa. I wouldn't bother with the ferry. So I figured no one else would, either."

She thought about that for a long time. "Only policemen could block off all the bridges."

"Yeah."

"If I thought it was policemen at the door, I wouldn't have run away."

"No."

"But you think it was policemen."

"Not necessarily. What I think is that you can give me some idea who they were. But we'll talk about that later."

"Not tonight. Tomorrow, maybe."

"We'll see."

We found Gavan's Hotel and went in to register. I figured it was easier if Ken and I were brothers and Mrs. Robinson and I were man and wife. We let it be known that we were from Toronto, on our way to the north woods to do some fishing. I had no idea if anyone ever went to the north woods to fish in August, but it seemed the thing to say at the time.

I assumed that the charade was just for the desk clerk, and Ken and I would share a room. That wasn't the way Ken and the clerk, who carried our bags upstairs, figured it. I found myself in the room with Mrs. Robinson, with Ken saying goodnight and going into the room next door.

I was awkward. I didn't know exactly what to do. She did all those female things, straightening out the curtains, turning on the lamp, testing the water in the washroom.

"I've got no clothes to wear, Mr. Duggan."

"No." I didn't know what else to say. I suppose that was the last moment I could have gone next door.

"Have you got pyjamas in that bag?"

"No."

She flopped on the bed. " 'No'? Is that all you can say?"

"No." We laughed together, and some of the tension was broken. I opened the club-bag, took out the last of the bottle of Toronto whiskey. "Want a drink?"

"That would be nice." We finished the bottle, saying nothing. She sat on the bed, I stood by the dresser. As she finished the last of her glass, she sighed. It was the sigh of the dead. She stood, walking towards me.

"Still want to pretend you're my boyfriend?"

I put down my glass and walked towards her.

"I've got two broken ribs and three cracked ribs." She laughed. "Won't be much of a boyfriend, then, will you?"

We fell to the bed, both laughing. I ignored the pain.

We lay together, her fingers tracing little circles on my bandages.

"You lied to me." I started, thinking she was serious. If anyone was a liar, it was her. Then I saw the smile on her face. That forced a smile from me.

"What did I lie about?"

"You said you were all thoughts and no action."

"If I recall correctly, I said I was all thoughts and 'little' action. There's a world of difference."

"That wasn't so little."

"No, it wasn't."

Suddenly, my eyes filled with tears. I felt foolish, wiping them angrily away. She had moved me so much, touching me deep inside. I never wanted to let her go. And I still wasn't sure that she wasn't a murderess. The worst part was that I knew she had touched me more deeply than I had touched her.

"Can I call you Pen, now?"

"If I can call you Phoebe." We laughed and lay together in silence.

I had a new hunger eating me up. "You got any cigarettes?"

"I never knew you to smoke."

"You haven't known me long."

"No. I've got no cigarettes." More silence. "Why do I feel I have known you for a long time?"

"I don't know, girl." The moment had suddenly passed, and I was restless.

"So, now I'm 'girl', and not 'Phoebe'!" Her instincts were immediate and unerring.

"It's an old term of endearment."

"It's an old term of dismissal."

"Don't be foolish." Nevertheless, I sat up and turned on the lamp. I couldn't help it. There were so many questions I wanted answered. I got up and put some clothes on. "Let's talk."

"You said it could wait until tomorrow."

"No, I said, 'We'll see'."

"That's the same thing."

"When my mother said, 'We'll see', she always meant, 'No'."

"When my mother said, 'We'll see', she always meant, 'Yes'."

"Nevertheless, I meant, 'We'll talk tonight'."

"Pen?"

"Yes?"

"You're ruining it. You're deliberately fighting against everything that's happened in the last hour. Why, Pen, why?"

"You're being foolish, girl." I was horrified. She was right. Even her use of my first name was irritating me.

"Pen?"

"Yes."

"Call me 'Phoebe'. Don't call me 'girl'."

"Okay. Phoebe."

"Pen?" I was becoming more and more irritated.

"Yes!"

"Call me 'Martha'. Don't call me 'Phoebe'."

I tucked my shirt into my pants, checked my reflection in the mirror, picked up the doorkey from the dresser.

"I'm going down for cigarettes. I'll be right back." She didn't say anything.

When I returned, all the lights were off and she was beneath the blankets, asleep, or feigning sleep. I turned all the lights on once more. She stirred and sat up.

"Okay, Martha, let's talk."

She reached over and took some of her clothes under the blanket with her, dressing out of my sight. She pushed the covers off her. She had her dress on. She bent down and picked up her stockings.

"I'm sorry, Pen, if I've pushed you too far. It's obvious that you don't want to talk to Martha. You want to talk to Mrs. Robinson. Okay, let's talk. Why don't you ask Mrs. Robinson your questions. Mr. Duggan." There wasn't even a trace of regret in her voice, only a reasoning that was ice-cold. I knew there weren't enough confessions in all the churches of the world to make up for the way I was acting now. I watched her pull on her stockings without saying a word. We seemed to be acting a ritual neither of us wanted but were forced to replay because they had been handed down from generation even unto generation. "Want another drink?" I had bought a bottle downstairs.

"No." She sat primly on the bed, hands folded on her lap.

"Want to talk?"

"I'd rather make love." Her answer shocked me, and I was non-plussed for a moment.

"Still?"

"Duggan, you're a right bastard. Did anyone tell you that you are a total phoney? You seem to be one thing, then you reveal your true self. You hurt other people so much. I hope that, before you die, you realize that. You think you are being so true to some idealization of yourself that you have, when all the time you are betraying your real self." The worst part was that I knew she was absolutely correct.

"I can't help being what I am."

"No. I suppose that's true. But I want you to know that on three occasions tonight I offered you a chance to open your heart, and you refused all three chances. I want you to know that I don't think you're an evil man, but you're not a good man, either. Now, ask your questions."

"I never said I was a good man."

"No. You did worse. You pretended you were a good man working under conditions that made it difficult to be good. The truth is, it's not the conditions that make it difficult, it's your own self that is morally neutral. Now, ask your questions."

"Don't tell me what I am or am not. You haven't known me long enough to find out."

"Ask your questions. I've said what I want to say about your goodness or lack of it."

"You made love to a man with his body all broken and bruised, and you didn't even have the curiosity to ask why he was in that shape. You don't care about me at all!"

"I already knew the answer. I didn't have to ask."

"You knew nothing."

"I knew this much: that you pitted your body against another in a moral battle that the opponent didn't even know he was fighting. So you took a physical beating, but won a moral victory. I didn't have to ask about that. I knew. And you refuse me credit for knowing without making you explain."

Things were moving way too fast. I didn't want her opening me up with a scalpel. I knew I had made a big mistake getting close to her. I took a drink. Then another. It seems I always made a big mistake when I got close to a woman. I just didn't know how to handle it. I always botched it. Goddamn it. Why must I always be tormented?

"Let's leave all that. We don't have much time. Let's try to figure things out. It that all right with you?"

"Whatever you say, Detective." She rose and poured a small bit of whiskey for herself. In the bathroom, she added water.

"Let's work backwards. Who do you think came knocking on your door tonight?"

"Someone thinks I know more than I do about poor Walter's suicide." Her eyes, soft in the lamplight, locked onto mine. "Believe me, Detective, I don't know anything."

"Okay. Another step backwards. How is it that Sergeant Carson convinced you to leave your hotel? And where did you go?"

"It was the Senator's idea, really. The three of us met in my hotel room, and he suggested I should leave and go where only the Mounties knew I was. It was, I'm afraid, one way to keep you from questioning me too closely. I agreed, partly because I didn't want you to find out that I wasn't home the night Walter. . .the night Walter died."

"I found out anyway."

"Yes."

"There were other reasons."

"Yes."

"What were they?"

"Walter was being forbidden by the government to testify in Washington. It wasn't his decision at all. I remember, only a week before he died, he told me, 'They won't let me go down'."

I had my own ideas what he might have meant by that statement, but I didn't say anything. I was pacing the floor, sipping from my glass. She was on the bed, sitting upright and nervously fingering hers.

"What else did he say?"

"Nothing much. He never told me much. I preferred it that way, if truth be known." I certainly was in favour of truth being known. It would certainly be a welcome change. "I knew that Walter had been invited – perhaps ordered is a better word – by the Americans to go to Washington, but not much more. He said that External was against his appearance at the committee. He said they were discussing postings as far away from America as possible. 'They won't let me go down', he said."

"Did he really want to go down to Washington?"

"No. He was deathly afraid of going. But I got the impression he felt it was something he had to face and if they had permitted it, he would have gone."

"Everyone else says he committed suicide because he didn't want to testify. 'Death before dishonour' is, I believe, the phrase used."

She laughed, a small, cynical laugh. "I'm sorry I laughed, but that's the title of the last chapter of one of Walter's chess books. It has to do with forsaking a clear stalemate in order to try to achieve victory through aggressiveness." That reminded me that someone had played chess with Robinson before he died. Someone not very good. The game had lasted less than ten moves, it looked like.

"Did you play chess with Walter the night he died?"

"No." I let it lie.

"When you left the hotel, where did you go?"

"I was staying at a friend's. Betty Cooper. Her husband is an executive with B.P. stationed in London. She's spending the summer all alone in a huge apartment. We were company for each other."

"The Senator, Carson, me, you, Betty Cooper, all knew where you were. Anyone else?"

"A few friends I phoned."

"Women friends?"

"Women friends."

"When we're finished here, maybe you could make a list of everyone who knew you were at the Cooper apartment. Everyone."

"Okay."

"Did Carson interview you at the apartment?"

"Yes. Three times, I think."

"What sort of questions? What was he most interested in?"

"Mostly he wanted to know about Walter's friends back in England before the war. Who they were, what their politics were, where they are now, that sort of thing."

That disappointed me. Carson was still trying to prove that Robinson was a security threat, even after his death.

"Did you know all that stuff?"

"I knew quite a bit. We have kept in touch with many of them. Mainly through Christmas cards, birthdays, things like that."

Now, that was interesting. Maybe Carson had a point, after all.

"Was he interested in anyone in particular?"

"No. He asked me the same questions about everyone. It gave me headaches sometimes, thinking so much."

"Did Walter know the scientist, Allan Nunn May?"

She gasped. "You, too! I told Sergeant Carson that neither one of us had met him. Walter's friends were writers, artists, other diplomats. He had no interest in science. Why is this Nunn so important, anyway?"

I didn't answer her questions. No, there was no way that Carson was stupid. He was on the track of something.

"Anyone else visit you at the apartment?"

"No."

"I'd like to go back to the photo of a woman I showed you once. I'm convinced there's a connection somewhere. Are you sure you've never seen her before?"

"I'm sure."

"Did Carson ask about her?"

"No. Never. He just asked about Walter's old friends."

"Okay. We'll let that go for now. Did Walter have any Soviet friends at all?"

"Not that I know of. He met Soviets at diplomatic functions, of course. We both did. But he wasn't particularly friendly with any of them."

"No Russian connection at all that you can think of."

"No. . .not, that is, unless you count John."

"John?"

"John Watkins. He's the Canadian ambassador to Russia. Walter and he are old friends. That's normal. It can't mean anything. But it's the only Russian connection I can think of."

"Hell. It's like swimming in pea soup."

"But why would you be looking for a Russian connection? Was that woman a Russian?"

"She's a dead Russian. But I can't find any connection. I must be wrong." I'd give up the idea a lot easier if she hadn't called me the night before she died.

"Can I sleep now?" I looked over at her. She was stretched out on the bed. She looked beat. I had already slept six hours. I wasn't tired.

"I'm sorry. Of course. Turn out the light. I'll sit up for awhile. I'm too tense to sleep."

"G'night, Pen," she whispered sleepily, reaching over to turn out the light. I sat a long time in the darkness.

CHAPTER 14

Three decades later, what I remember the most clearly about that summer was the next three or four hours. It's funny to remember remembering so well. I sat in the dark, thinking. I went over every little detail of the past eight days, remembered a movement, a glance, the exact way a word was spoken. I remembered whether a man's shoes were polished or not, whether a woman's stocking seam was straight or not. I remembered the exact sound of a match being struck, the sound of high heels on a tile floor. I remembered the smell of draft beer mixed with other tavern smells, I remembered the smell of perfume on a scented neck.

Perhaps it was the sensory deprivation that made everything flood back so clear in memory. There were no lights on. There was no sound except the soft breathing from the bed.

Around four in the morning, I had a glimmer of what the truth might be. I admit now I had only a surface knowledge, but it was enough. The senseless made sense again. I knew proving it was going to be impossible.

When at last I was satisfied I knew at least a little bit of the truth, I drained my glass and lay on the bed, fully clothed.

"I love you, Martha," I whispered, not even knowing if that was the truth or not.

"I know, Pen," she whispered, holding the blankets open for me to slide under.

My brother Ken was a wonder. We met early for breakfast the next morning, and he didn't ask a single question, neither about

Martha nor the investigation. He must have been straining with curiosity, but he asked not a question. That's what brothers are for, I guess.

We made our plans for the day. I was going to miss my eight o'clock appointment with the Chief. I had already twice disobeyed orders, both by having contact with Martha and by leaving town.

Ken got off the hook easily, by phoning his wife and pledging her to secrecy except to say, if anyone asked, that he was on an out-of-town construction job.

After breakfast, we drove the truck back to Ottawa.

"Father, we seek sanctuary."

Father Scanlon was still at breakfast when we walked into the rectory. He stood, wiping egg from his chin with a large napkin.

"Now, don't go makin' fun of an old priest, Pendrick." There was a gleam in his eyes, and a smile on his face.

"No joke, Father. You remember the man who died in a fall at the Chateau Laurier? Well, this is his wife, Martha. Martha Robinson, meet Father Scanlon, a rapscallion priest of the old school." They shook hands, Father Scanlon retreating into the graciousness that was his only attitude towards women.

"Of course, of course, my dear. Pendrick has said so many nice things about you." I had done no such thing.

"And you know my brother Kenneth."

"Did I not baptize his first-born?"

"Surprised you remembered, Father."

"Not at all, my boy. You lived on Clarence Street before you moved to Eastview."

"That's right, Father."

"Now, what's this talk of sanctuary all about?"

"To solve the case, Father, Mrs. Robinson must stay out of sight for awhile." I put it into movie terms, so Father Scanlon could get into the spirit of the thing. "I hoped that she could stay here for awhile."

"A beautiful widow in the home of a priest, whatever are you thinking, Pendrick?"

"A wee bit of scandal would do wonders for your reputation,

Father. Why, Sunday Mass would be overflowing for months to come."

Martha laughed. Father Scanlon beamed. He was in his element now, acting like Barry Fitzgerald to my Bing Crosby in *Going My Way*.

"Seriously, my son, I'll help our police in any way I can. But surely the poor woman will be ready to leave here before midnight, I hope." Martha laughed once more. Father Scanlon was turning our problems into a vaudeville act. It lightened everyone's tension.

"I'll call back later to tell you." I turned to Martha. "Now, don't let him try to convert you. He was trained as a missionary, and he's always trying to keep in practice."

"I won't, Detective." The smile in her eyes betrayed the formality in her voice. Father Scanlon sidled up to me.

"She can earn her keep. I was planning to spend the morning polishing the silverware. She can lend a hand." He put a hand on my arm and whispered. "Seriously, Pen, I really do hope she won't have to spend the night here." His eyes widened. "Why, she's no luggage with her."

"I'm not sure, Father. I'll let you know."

Outside, I looked at the list Martha had written for me. There were three names and telephone numbers on it. I was sure the names were useless. I crumpled the paper and threw it into the gutter before I climbed into the truck.

"Where to?"

"Wellington and Bank. RCM Police Headquarters. . .and Ken, thanks for not asking questions. I'll tell you the whole story later."

"Oh, that's okay. Just so long as you pay for my gas."

"Jesus, you're right. I'm almost broke, myself. Look, Ken, here's the key to my house. In the bible on the mantle, there's a few bucks. Pay yourself for the gas and take an extra hundred for me. I can't go there right now. If anyone tries to stop you, tell them I gave you permission to go inside to check that everything's all right. But you haven't seen me since Saturday night. Got it?"

"An extra hundred? How much you got around the house?"

"I'm not sure. Around two hundred. But I dip into it for

groceries and things."

"You keep two hundred dollars in the bible. Christ, Pen, any cop would tell you that's a terrible place to hide money. It's the first place a burglar would look."

"Who's going to burgle a policeman's house?"

"My God, so much money. You know, if I want two dollars I have to consult with Rita."

"When this is all over, come into business with me. You'll be able to hide two hundred dollars in your bible, then. Maybe even three hundred."

"Maybe I will, Pen, maybe I will. But I'll find a better hiding place." At the next red light he turned to me. "You're in big trouble, eh?"

"I'm always in trouble, you know that."

"Who'd try to stop me from going into your house?"

"The police."

"That's what I thought. Jesus Christ!"

"You'll come with the hundred when I call."

"Of course."

We drove in silence to Mountie headquarters. I jumped out, waved goodbye to Ken. Well, here goes nothing. Or everything.

"Detective Duggan, well, well, well!" Sergeant Carson was in civvies this time. He was not smiling. We were in the same interview room. It looked exactly the same.

"Sergeant Carson. Long time no see."

"A lot of water under the bridge since the last time we spoke."

"We were attending a funeral, as I recall."

"You know that every constable in Ottawa has orders to pick you up on sight."

"I thought as much. But, as you can see, I slipped the cordon and made it into the horsemen's headquarters."

"If I don't turn you in, I'll be a headless horseman."

"There's the phone, Sergeant. You know the number."

He sighed deeply. He sat down, running his hand through his hair. He obviously liked the feel of the bristles. He straightened his tie.

"What do you want, Duggan?"

"You, me, the Senator. All together in one room. Doors closed, windows locked. Phone off the hook."

"That's impossible. You're *persona non grata* anywhere in this town except in a jail cell."

"You, me, the Senator, right now."

"Where's Mrs. Robinson?"

"You, me, the Senator."

"If you go to jail, she'll have to surface sometime."

"That your boys who bungled her pick-up?"

"My boys." Again, he sighed deeply.

"They should have done it by the book. She would have come in. They frightened her."

"They don't train them like they used to."

"Too much horseshit."

"Yeah, too much horseshit."

"You, me, the Senator."

"What makes you think you can give me orders?"

"I've got the star witness in this case hidden away. What have you got?"

"Wait here." He left the room. I smoked the second cigarette of the day. I hoped when it was all over I'd be able to quit again.

He returned fifteen minutes later. I was on my third cigarette of the day.

"I didn't know you smoked."

"You haven't known me very long."

"Where is she, Duggan?"

"She's in a safe place. She'll show herself when she knows what you want her for. And, if you've got a valid warrant."

"She's a material witness."

"To a suicide."

"Duggan, I'll never know why you fight so hard."

"Nor will I. It's just my nature, that's all."

"Let's take a walk."

"Good lad." I retrieved my hat, and we walked into the morning sunshine. "Where we going?"

"The senate." We walked in silence for awhile. "You really kill your wife, Duggan?"

"Of course not. You give them my army record, Carson?"

"Of course not. I don't have that kind of pull."

"Superintendent Francis?"

"Or maybe even higher up than that. Takes someone with connections to Veterans' Affairs Department."

"The Senator."

"Maybe. Or someone in External. Doubt we'll ever find out."

"No, I guess not." I was sure he was right.

"Why'd she call you?"

"Guess I was the only one she could trust."

"She didn't know it was us. Why didn't she call me?"

"She likes my honest face."

"She can't be trusted to tell a word of the truth, Duggan."

"I'm sure you're right, my boy. Still and all, she's a pretty face."

"She is that."

We were ushered into the Senator's office. He didn't rise from behind his desk.

"No calls, Constance."

"No, Senator."

We sat, uninvited, in two chairs arranged around his desk. There was something wrong. It took a moment to figure out that the Senator had a platform behind his desk, so that when he sat in his chair he looked taller, or we looked smaller. It was a neat trick. I filed it away. It might do wonders when interrogating a suspect.

"Detective Duggan thought we should talk, Senator."

"Talk, then."

"Is it eleven yet?" Just then, the Peace Tower clock chimed the quarter-past. "Eleven-fifteen? I guess the bar is open." I made myself a rye and ginger ale. "Anyone else?" There were no takers.

"You're very pushy, Detective. Perhaps you might inform us what makes you so confident, considering one phone call would put you behind bars." The Senator began to rise, then thought better of it. He turned to Carson. "What does he want?"

Carson shrugged. "Beats me." They both stared at me.

"First of all, this set-up stinks."

They both looked non-plussed. I guess they couldn't figure which set-up I meant.

"What set-up?" They spoke in unison.

"This. A seat in the senate. Money. Power. Prestige. All this for a piece of shit who should have been shovelled into the sewer a long time ago." The Senator turned red. His eyes bulged. He wasn't used to people talking like this. I was dead already, so I didn't care. Carson rose to his feet.

"Careful, Duggan. I think I can take you." He looked ready to try. I focussed my attention on the Senator.

"Never met me before, did you, Senator? But I remember you. I remember you well."

"What are you talking about?" He was both angry and non-plussed.

"About eighteen years ago. Don't you remember what happened eighteen years ago?"

"I'm afraid I don't." He slumped a little in his chair.

"I arrested your son-in-law. I would have arrested your daughter if I could have convinced the Chief in those days."

"You're impertinent!" He was sitting straight in his chair now. Carson was leaning towards me, rigid with tenseness.

"I know he was working for you."

"That's a libelous statement, Detective."

"Slanderous."

"What?"

"Libel is written. Slander spoken."

Carson broke in. "Do we have to rehash ancient history?"

"I just want the Senator to know that I'm aware of how he made his money. And I'm not impressed." I tossed off the rest of my drink. Carson stood and walked towards me.

"Okay, you're a tough cop in your own way. A smalltown way. We're convinced. Let's move along." I was worried Carson might take a poke at me, and in my condition it would be the death of me. But I was after the Senator.

"I also shot one of your drivers. On the Interprovincial Bridge. Remember that?" The Senator said nothing, glaring at me. "Also, I arrested about fifty of your girls when I was a vice cop. I sent them packing across the bridge. You finally got the message. We've always had enough scum of our own over here, without you contributing."

"I don't know what you're talking about."

"Look, you're talking to a Senator here. Have some respect." Carson was pandering now. I was in a cold fury.

"Respect? Respect for a bootlegger, a whoremonger, a thief? Respect? Contempt is closer to my feelings."

The Senator came from behind his desk and stood glaring down on me. I crossed my legs, smiling.

"Sergeant Carson, I think that now we should have this man arrested. Please call the local police."

"I'm tempted to agree with you." Carson stood with the Senator. "I don't know how you keep your badge with that Boy Scout attitude."

The Senator was bent almost double trying to yell in my face. "And you're wrong! My son-in-law was acquitted. It was clearly a case of police harassment."

I turned to Carson. "Tell him to shut the fuck up and get his stinking face away from mine or I'll slap him silly." I really didn't think I could slap anyone silly, but I thought it sounded good.

"And now, police brutality." The Senator talked a big game, but I noticed he took his face away from mine. Carson stood between him and me.

"Enough, Duggan. I guess this was a mistake." I turned to the Senator.

"No mistake. He may have been acquitted, but I bet it cost you a bundle. It costs a lot of money to buy a prosecutor and a judge. Maybe, for a guy as greedy as you, that's even better." I stood up to make another drink. The Senator thought I was about to tackle him and cowered. Carson put his hand on my shoulder.

"Enough, enough! Let's get down to brass tacks."

"Okay, okay. So long as I'm not expected to respect him because he's legitimate now. Jesus!" I made the drink.

The Senator sat down in his chair again. Carson shook his head from side to side in bewilderment. "That's better. But I really don't know if we have anything to talk about. You two screaming at each other is getting on my nerves. Maybe we should adjourn this little meeting."

The Senator was calmed down now, rubbing his hands

together slowly. "No, No, Sergeant. Maybe now that Mr. Duggan has vented his spleen, we can get to the hub of the matter. Sergeant, why not pour us both a small brandy? I'm going to enjoy the next ten minutes." He smiled, still rubbing his hands.

Carson made two new drinks. I massaged my aching ribs. The Senator rubbed his hands together.

"Shall I continue? Shall I tell you what has been happening in your absence, Detective?" I really felt like slapping his mouth, but I kept still.

"You owe me at least that much."

"I owe you nothing, but I'll tell you anyway, because I'll enjoy it so much. First of all, the result of Sergeant Carson's investigation of the death of Mr. Robinson is that he committed suicide."

"Surprise me."

"Secondly, as soon as Mrs. Robinson is found, she will be returned to England."

"I'm still not surprised."

"Third, certain of Mr. Robinson's friends and associates will no longer have government employment."

"That's better."

"Fourth, Sergeant Carson will no doubt be promoted for his brilliant handling of this investigation."

"Let the chips fall where they may."

"And finally, the story you want. Why we're so insistent on doing things our way."

"Yeah, finally." I handed my glass to Carson. I was getting a bit tipsy, but it seemed the thing to do. The Senator was obviously enjoying himself. Carson wasn't crazy about that, so he took up the story himself, while pouring drinks.

"The truth is, Robinson was a security risk."

"I've never been convinced of that."

"No matter. He covered for obvious subversives. I've no proof he himself ever did anything traitorous..."

"'Traitorous'? Isn't that a pretty strong word?"

"Traitorous. It took three investigations, but I've finally found the evidence. I can show it to you, if you wish."

My heart was getting heavier. "No, that's okay."

"Now we get to the part you won't like."

"I was afraid of that."

"His hand was in the cookie jar. The Americans know about it. They invite him to Washington. External won't let him go."

"Mrs. Robinson confirms that." Now, it was between Carson and me. The Senator didn't count any more.

"Here's the plan: They don't send him to Washington. They defend him in public. Then they boot him out of the diplomatic service. He's officially cleared in public, but behind the scenes everyone knows he's guilty. Not only is his career over, but he'll never get another job except as dishwasher or cabdriver. So, what does he do?"

"He takes a high dive." My voice was barely over a whisper.

"Right. Now, if Robinson was a stronger man, he'd tell External to take a flying leap and go down to Washington. He'd try to bluff his way through and save his career. But you know how they browbeat witnesses down there. They'd make mincemeat of him. And in public. And he knows it. He'd be worse off than ever."

"Tough choices."

"Choice one, he loses his career. Choice two, he also loses his career. Choice three, he loses his life."

"You put it so poetically, Carson."

"I don't know about poetry, Duggan, but it does have symmetry. Admit it. You're beat. The guy jumped. He cracked under pressure, and who can blame him?"

"Okay, I admit there's a certain sense to it." I considered standing up, but I wasn't sure that I wouldn't weave, so I didn't even try. "But what about Mrs. Robinson? Why the hide-and-seek game? Why the pressure? Why send her to England?" The Senator was laughing openly now.

"Another cognac, Sergeant. My, I'm certainly enjoying this." I glared him into silence. Carson made the drinks, refilling mine while he was at it.

"You sure you're a hot-shot homicide cop? Can't you figure it out? Take your time." The Senator and Carson clinked their ponies while I thought.

I shouldn't drink so much. I know that. My thoughts were cloudy. It took awhile to clear my brain. I remembered the night before and all my memories. I had thought these terrible thoughts at three in the morning. I had rejected them then, but the soft breathing from the bed may have had an influence.

"She was one of the 'obvious subversives'." I felt an emptiness I knew I'd never fill again.

"He's slow, but he's thorough." I heard the Senator's voice as through a fog. Were I more sober, I would have strangled him then. It was just as well. My most traitorous thoughts of last night had been confirmed. Now Carson was leaning over me.

"Again, I'll show you the proof, if you want."

"That's okay. No thanks."

"Duggan, this can't come out into the public. As a matter of fact, none of the story can. The government will be satisfied if she goes back to England."

"Where she belongs." The Senator still wasn't endearing himself to me.

"Okay, I'll accept what you've said. I wasn't so wrong in my own figuring. So, what happens the night of the suicide?"

"If you've already figured things out so far, this is where I'll bet you go wrong. She doesn't help him out the window at all. Okay, maybe she knows what he plans to do and she doesn't stop him. She says, 'I'm going to bed, do whatever you have to do.' It may not be nice, but it's no crime."

"I liked that woman." Sometimes, I'm given to understatement.

"She's a diplomat's wife. Being likeable is part of the training." The Senator held up his glass for a refill while speaking.

"No reason to like her any more or less. Like I said, she didn't commit any crime that night." Carson was being remarkably forgiving.

"No, I'm sure you're right." I was suddenly very sober. I was as equally humble. "Only one thing I can't figure. You had done all those investigations of Robinson. You knew about his wife from day one. Why try to brush me? Why not just tell me the story?"

The Senator smiled and walked towards me. "I'm afraid it's a simple case of human pride. Sergeant Carson thought he could browbeat you." He gave Carson a murderous look, which Carson returned. "He thought he wouldn't have to tell you the story, that he would match wits with you and emerge victorious."

"And the Senator agreed." They exchanged more looks.

"Okay. I'm out. You've convinced me. He committed suicide. That's enough pressure for any man to crack under."

"By the way, a bit more for you." The Senator was enjoying himself now. "Mrs. Robinson was one of the more famous adultresses on the diplomatic circuit."

I had a little pride left. "I had already figured that out for myself. Robinson wasn't the most loving of husbands. But that's all right. It didn't make me like her any less." I picked up my hat from the floor and stood up. I didn't weave a bit. "Okay, you guys were right and I was wrong. I'll see you soon."

"Where are you going?"

"I'm not sure right now. I'll be in touch later. There's still half a story missing. About that Voscovitch woman."

"That's another long story. It involves American security agents."

"I'm not surprised."

"What about Mrs. Robinson?"

"If she returns to her hotel room, will you promise to leave her alone until tomorrow morning?"

They looked at each other. The Senator shrugged. Carson rubbed his crewcut. "Sounds all right. So long as you promise no tricks in the meantime."

"No tricks. I'll set it up right now. But, if either of you doublecrosses me, you're dead. I mean it. If you don't believe I can do it, read my army record." I figured I might as well get some use out of those damned files. The Senator blanched. Carson finished his drink, eyeing me thoughtfully. I phoned the rectory. "Mrs. Robinson, please."

Father Scanlon was on the line. "Duggan, me lad, your charge is safe as an angel in heaven. And what a woman she is! I'll perform the wedding ceremony myself. Here she is, now."

"Mrs. Robinson? Duggan, here. I'm assured that if you return to your room at the Chateau Laurier, you will be safe from harm. Do not return to the apartment, go to the hotel. Is that clear?"

"You sound so strange, is there anything the matter, Pen?"

"The hotel. I'll be in touch later. If you're short of taxi fare, borrow two dollars from your host. I'll repay him."

"Pen, what on earth is the matter? You sound as if you're a million miles away."

"Just do as I say." I hung up the phone.

CHAPTER 15

The tourists were in season on Parliament Hill, snapping kodaks of the scarlet Mounties on guard for thee.

It was a perfect summer's day, the red ensign flag flapping lazily in a mild breeze.

I had my next two stops figured out, hoping I'd be able to walk the streets without some constable getting cocky enough to try to take me into the station. I'd get there in my own time.

I thought I hid it pretty well, but they had thrown me for a loop with their idea that Martha was a commie. Not that I hadn't considered that possibility myself. But I wish she had told me. "Walter never told me anything, Pen, and that's the way I preferred it." Nuts to her, and to all women.

I walked up to Laurier and over to the public library. Carnegie's bid to achieve forgiveness for his theft and avarice. The hell with him, too.

I laughed when I found what I was looking for. Why does everybody always think Duggan is so stupid? Maybe I overdo the Irish background thing. Maybe a big Irish cop is supposed to be stupid, and nobody can get that image out of his mind. Still and all, I don't think I have very much of an Irish accent, just a hint of a soft brogue, that's all, and maybe an odd turn of phrase sometimes, but not what you'd call a real accent. Maybe I should wear glasses. At my age, I'll probably have to start wearing them pretty soon, anyhow. I could court the intellectual look. People may take me for less of a fool. Although I must admit I do act the fool sometimes. Damn everybody anyway.

There he was, staring out of a photo at me, the American ambassador with his wife, attending the annual Maycourt Ball. He bore no resemblance at all to the man I had been talking to in the embassy.

Why didn't he just tell me he was the security chief or CIA man, or whatever he was? I wouldn't have minded. Did they really think I wouldn't bother checking up? After I mulled it over for awhile, that's what I figured they really thought. Well, a picture is worth lots of words, so I ripped it out of the newspaper, although I knew I wasn't supposed to.

A pleasant walk across the Laurier bridge and I was close to the station. I met Ti-Luc Beaupré, who ran a few girls out of the old Lasalle Hotel on Dalhousie Street, but we didn't exchange anything more than glances. Ti-Luc has never forgiven me for telling a judge that I saw him taking money from one of his girls, and he got two years for it.

Ti-Luc knows better than to accept money when there's anyone else around. But I'm sure his spell down in the Kingston Penitentiary did him good. I know it did the city good.

"Hiya, Chief."

I smiled and moved towards him in the hallway, cutting off his retreat.

"Duggan!"

"Sorry I'm late. Slept in this morning."

"Late? Goddamn right you're late." He didn't sound in a forgiving mood.

"Must have been the pills the doctor gave me." I tried to work on his sympathetic nature.

"You know you've been on the bulletin since nine this morning?"

"Well, I'm here now. What do you want me to do?" I thought I was being extremely friendly, given the circumstances.

"We've had your brother in for the last hour."

"Ken? Why bother him? He doesn't know nothing."

"That's what he keeps saying."

"What else is new?" The Chief kept trying to edge around me. I guess he had important business elsewhere.

"Wallace and Sherman are handing your file over to the crown prosecutor this afternoon. We'll let you know what he says."

"He'll say you got no case. Excuse me, I'll go see about Ken." I turned away. I always like having the last word.

I stuck my head into the interrogation room. "Ken? Tell these people your brother has shown up. While you're at it, tell them you been lying for the past hour, that you knew where I was all the time. Hah, hah!" Childish, Duggan, childish.

I sat at my desk. Bruno had kept it clean. There were no messages. Bruno was nowhere in sight. It wouldn't do to ask anyone where he was, they wouldn't tell me anyway. For my sins, and for fear of Internal Affairs, I had been sent to Coventry.

Ken came over, flanked by Wallace and Sherman. I looked him over carefully.

"Ken. Hi. They hurt you? If they did..."

"If we did, you won't do nothin', Duggan." Wallace was feeling as miserable as ever, it sounded like.

Ken shook his head. "No, they didn't touch me."

Sherman waved his hands in the air, wrinkling his nose in distaste. "Jesus! Smell the air in here. He's been drinking already."

"Drunk or sober, I'm still ten times the investigator you are, Wallace. So piss off."

"Wallace, sir," Sherman growled.

I said nothing. They glared at me. As a parting shot, Sherman yelled over his shoulder, "We get the warrant tomorrow, Duggan. Then we'll see who's the best investigators."

"You won't get no warrant." They turned.

"Wanna bet?"

"What you got to bet with, Wallace? I bet my life." With a dismissive wave, they continued on their way. Probably off to beat up on some old lady. I had got in the last word again.

Ken passed me the hundred. I peeled off a twenty.

"A tip. For good service. Don't tell Rita." At first, I thought he might refuse it, but he thought better of that idea.

"Thanks."

"Get lost now. I got work to do. See ya on your birthday."

"Okay. Be careful, Pen. You're the only brother I got." Yeah, yeah. Ken always was a sap for that family stuff. I waved him out of the room.

I couldn't find Bruno anywhere. I phoned every place I thought he might be, before I gave up. Maybe he had a new girlfriend.

I tried Duckworth, over at External. After having the call forwarded a couple of times, he came onto the line.

"Detective Duggan? I haven't heard from you in a long time. Look, let me get back to my office and I'll call you right back."

Duckworth's 'right back' was about twenty minutes later. "What can I do for you, Detective?"

"Anything new with our Russian friends?"

"Actually, quite a few things."

"Yeah?"

"Yeah. One of your friends, Nikola Cherniak, has been recalled to Moscow."

"That's big news, all right. That will keep him out of my clutches."

"Be careful, Detective. Diplomatic immunity will keep all Soviets out of your clutches."

"Yeah, yeah, just joking." I wasn't joking, but he didn't have to know that. "I suppose they're raising hell about Voscovitch's murder, eh?"

"You'd think so. But, the truth is, they're not. They've referred to it officially as 'the accident' to comrade Voscovitch."

"I'm not surprised. Okay, I know you're not supposed to know this, but tell me: was Voscovitch some sort of agent, NKVD or KGB or whatever it is? Unofficially, of course."

"Of course. Officially, the Soviet Union has no security agents of any kind in Canada. However, if you asked me my opinion, I'd say she was probably KGB."

"Don't tell me. And Krupotkin was her boss."

"I shouldn't think so. Far more likely that Cherniak was. Or else Krutov. He's the chauffeur."

"But that's crazy!"

"No, not really. Officially, Krupotkin is boss as third secretary, but quite often it's the chauffeur, or the translator, or the messenger who's really in charge, the one with the direct line to Moscow."

"Trust commies to turn the natural order upside down."

"Now that you mention it, it is rather sly and cynical."

"Yeah. Listen, can I admit I lied to you?"

"Actually, it would be quite refreshing. In the diplomatic service, we're quite used to being lied to. Comes with the territory."

"I didn't exactly lie, I just didn't tell you the way I was figuring things out in my own mind."

"I'm not a mindreader, Detective. Why don't you give me an inkling as to how your mind works."

"I've got an idea I can't get rid of that the death of Voscovitch and the death of Robinson are connected."

"Sounds strange to me."

"Yeah, to me too. Sometimes I think maybe I just want them to be connected so if one is solved, the other will be, too."

"It would make your life easier."

"Yeah. What I want to ask is this: do you know anything about Voscovitch's past postings that would put her and Robinson together, like maybe they had an affair or something?"

"Now, Detective, that's going too far. In the first place, Robinson wasn't the sort of man to have affairs, and in the second place, if he ever was tempted he would make sure it was with someone who had absolutely no connection to a foreign embassy. It would be worth his career to have an affair with a KGB agent. The whole idea is preposterous."

"Okay, I'll back off that one. How about if they just were posted in the same place at the same time. Forget about an affair."

"I have no information that would place them in the same city at the same time."

"That sounds like a weaselly diplomatic way of not really answering the question."

"You're pushing, Detective. I don't deserve that."

"You're right. I'm sorry. Forget I said it. Try this one: was Voscovitch a chess expert, by any chance?"

There was a long pause on the line.

"Most Russians of good education are at least passable chess players. There's nothing in her dossier to suggest she was an expert."

"You keep cutting me off at the pass. I'll back off and ask the widest question I can think of: do you know of any possible connection between Voscovitch and Robinson?"

"There's nothing I know that would suggest the remotest connection."

"Oh, well. One step forward, twenty-seven back. So you really think this chauffeur could be the head KGB man, eh?"

"It's possible. No more than that."

"Okay, just a couple more questions. Last time I heard, the Russians were saying the dead woman wasn't Voscovitch at all. How'd they get out of that one?"

"A nice bit of fancy footwork. Krupotkin was so overcome when he saw her that his memory was blurred. Upon reflection, he realized that she really was who you said she was."

"Makes me wonder which story is the real one. Okay, what about the diplomatic notes, they still floating around accusing Duggan of all and sundry?"

"I'm afraid the charge of police brutality is still going ahead. As soon as the paperwork is organized. I'd say you're safe for another six months."

"Thanks. If I'm lucky, the chauffeur will be recalled to Moscow, too."

"I wouldn't be surprised. It would still be on your dossier, though."

"On my dossier, it would get lost among all the others."

Duckworth laughed. "Sounds like quite a file. Maybe we should have a drink sometime, and you can tell me your life story."

"You know, Mr. Duckworth, that doesn't sound half bad. My life story wouldn't be so interesting, but maybe we could exchange fishing stories and other lies."

"Good idea, Detective, give me a call sometime."

"I will. Goodbye, now." I knew I'd never give Duckworth a call. He probably knew it, too.

Goddamn it. I had that bastard chauffeur in my clutches and I let him slip away. I was in no shape to tackle him now, so he was having the last laugh on me. Oh, well. Right now, I'd bet a million dollars he was the one conked Voscovitch on the head. And no chance of even getting close to proving it. Mother of God, why do I keep screwing things up?

If I had any sense, I'd forget the connection between Voscovitch and Robinson. If only she hadn't called me the night before she died and mentioned him specifically.

Now that I think on it, yesterday I was accusing the Americans of killing her, today it's the Russians. Admit it, Duggan, you're floundering and the water keeps rising.

Bruno finally showed up. "Whatcha doin' here, Duggan?" he growled, maybe making a bit of an act for the rest of the lads.

"Waitin' for you, Bruno."

"Let's go somewhere else and talk," he says, looking uncomfortable.

"Afraid to be seen in the station with me?"

"That's not it at all, Duggan. The walls have ears."

After only a little debate, we retired to the Albion. There were a dozen or fifteen policemen there, who studiously ignored us. They'd feel silly when I was re-instated, I was thinking. Even the lawyers were keeping their distance. That reminded me, maybe I better find myself an attorney, one with a good lawyer's name like Goldbloom or Steinberg. I never trusted lawyers with names like O'Malley or Callaghan. Those are good names for policemen or aldermen, but they don't impress judges. I figured I'd leave it until tomorrow.

"What's new, Bruno?"

"Well, I did like the Chief asked. I sent the files on over to Superintendent Francis. But I made a Gestetner copy for you. Jeez, Duggan, they was mighty thin files."

"The Chief knew that. He was playing by the book."

"Don't know how you ever solved a single case, sittin' over here all day and never writin' nothin' down in the file. Don't make sense."

"Anything else new?"

"Them two from Internal had me in for a chit-chat. I told 'em I wasn't even on the force when you...when your wife died." That wasn't quite true. Bruno had been a patrolman for about six months when Lucille had died. I should know. But I let it pass. "They tried to talk about the two cases the Chief gave me, but I told them that wasn't part of their investigation. They wasn't too happy."

"I'm not surprised."

"I went by your place this morning when you didn't show up at the station. You weren't there."

"No, I wasn't." He didn't press it.

"There was a squad car outside, about half-way up the block. Couple of kids in it."

"My official escort service. For years I've been asking for my own squad car, and they finally give me one when I'm on suspension."

"I called Ed Lukowicz and brought him up to date. He was real sorry. He thinks you're a great guy."

"So do I. But no one else seems to agree."

We spent the better part of the afternoon talking about this and that. At the end of it, I didn't feel any closer to any answers than I did when we walked in.

Eventually, we had to leave. Bruno had his own case he was working on. I gave him the benefit of my advice on how to handle it, and we waved good-bye to each other on the corner.

I walked over to the Chateau Laurier. Time to call on my star witness.

"My bedroom is being painted."

The desk clerk was a young woman with a nice smile, a crooked nose, a pair of gold earrings and large breasts. It might seem funny to notice her breasts right off, but the rest of her body was hidden by the counter. She smiled her nice smile and sort of whispered, "I can't stand the smell of fresh paint."

"Neither can I. That's why I need a room." I figured that, since I was still hoping for a reimbursement sometime in the future, I might as well spend a few more bucks. And I wanted to be nearby, in case things started jumping. Maybe I'd even start them jumping myself. It's been known to happen.

I filled in the card. She looked at it carefully. "You're a policeman?"

"Can't a policeman get a room, same as a private citizen?"

"Of course. You ... you're not on duty, are you, I mean on a case or anything."

"Of course not, I'm just hiding away from paint fumes."

She smiled. It was still a nice smile. She handed me my room key, but didn't call for a bellman. Probably noticed I had no luggage. "For some reason, I didn't think you looked like a policeman."

"That's the nicest thing anybody's said to me in a month of Sundays."

She laughed again, making her earrings tinkle. "I bet."

"Am I eligible for any kind of discount? Old-age discount or something?"

"You don't look like an old-age pensioner to me."

"I bet you say that to all the old fogies."

In the end, she gave me a business rate. I paid in advance. She looked at the key. "Room 507. Is there anything about that number I should remember?"

My, my, my. Duggan the lady killer strikes again. Where were they all thirty years ago, when I was young and full of spark? My smile wasn't as nice as hers, but I tried. "I'm afraid I can't think of anything." She didn't look all that disappointed. I took myself to the elevators.

Room 507 was not nearly as nice as the rooms on the seventh floor, but it would do in a pinch. It seemed to have everything a hotel room needed except a nice view. This one looked out onto the stone walls of the department store opposite.

I called Martha. "I'm two floors down from you. Why not come visit?"

She had a parcel in her hand when she entered. "Close your eyes and pull down your pants."

"What?"

She laughed brightly. At least she was in a good mood. "When I was in school, I had a girlfriend who always tried to shock people, and she used to say that to all the fellows."

"I bet she was real popular."

"That she was." Her eyes clouded over with more seriousness. "Okay. Close your eyes and hold out your hand, if that's the way you want it."

It was a bottle of Canadian Club. Everyone in the world seemed to notice Duggan's drinking problem. Not that I thought of it as a problem, myself, more like a hobby. Well, another wee drop wouldn't do any harm.

I sat her down, drink in hand. "Let's talk."

She shook her head wearily from side to side. "What are we going to do, Pen?"

"We're going to talk and talk and talk until I know everything there is to know."

"Is that what investigation is, just talk?"

"I'm afraid that's ninety percent of it."

"Just like diplomacy."

"Yeah."

"I really got along well with Father Scanlon." I guess she was trying to change the subject.

"He seemed to like you all right, too."

"You were right. My conversion to Catholicism came up in conversation."

"What did you say?"

"I said I'd think about it. He seemed to think you and I were—what did he call it?—sparking."

"Well, we may have lit a few sparks in the night, but I don't think we're exactly aflame."

"Why do you think that is, Pen?"

"Dunno."

"Liar."

"I guess we're very different kinds of people."

"Well, at least you're not calling me 'girl' anymore."

"I think it's a perfectly acceptable form of address. My father used it all the time. In a most affectionate way."

"Yes?"

"Yes. 'Are my socks darned, girl?' he'd ask. Or, 'You know, girl, we should repaint the house this summer.'"

"I had a friend once, in England, called me 'girl' all the time. Trouble was, he called every other woman 'girl', too. I guess that kind of took the intimacy out of it. Made you feel sort of replaceable."

"Well, I won't use it any more. Okay?"

She smiled softly. "Okay."

"I saw the Senator and Carson this morning."

"Yes?"

"Why didn't you tell me?"

"Tell you what?"

I sighed deeply. It was going to be a long conversation. "That you were one of those subversives they were always going on about."

"Is that what they think?"

"I'm afraid so."

"Well, they're wrong. The whole idea is ridiculous."

"They claim to have proof. They wouldn't say that unless they could back it up."

"They're wrong. I'm no more a communist than you are."

"Well, we'll see. What do you think makes them think the way they do?"

"I don't know." She paced the room, trying to decide, no doubt, how much to tell me. "They're probably talking about the Spanish Civil War. I helped with a committee to assist the International Brigades. But everyone else was doing that in those days. It was the thing to do. And that was before I met Walter, even."

"That's a good start."

She sat on the bed, her shoulders sagging. "I suppose they know about Viktor."

"Viktor?"

"He was a friend I had. In Poland."

"What about him?"

"I'm sure I don't know. They must think of him as a spy or something. But nothing could be further from the truth. He was an army officer. He had been stationed in England during the war, fighting with the Polish Free Forces. We got along well. That's all."

"That's all? An affair with a communist army officer? Did it never occur to you that he might be an agent of some kind?"

"You're wrong! They're all wrong. It had nothing to do with that sort of thing."

"So there was no pillow talk, no gossip about who was being transferred where, who was missing from Cracow for a couple of weeks, who was having an affair with someone they shouldn't. Jesus, no wonder they suspect you. And of course, your husband wouldn't say anything about it, even if he knew."

"Don't talk like that! It wasn't like you think."

Finally, I exploded. I grabbed her by the shoulders and shook her. I stopped almost immediately, afraid I'd go too far.

"You silly bitch! You pretend to be so innocent, when all the time you're playing with fire. There's more—I know there's more. God alone knows what English-Russian friendship society you belonged to, what messages you delivered for your so-called lovers, what lies have been spoken and deceits uttered. I dare you, tell me there's nothing else they've got on you."

She said nothing.

We sat in silence for a long time. I drank. She did nothing.

After a long time, she went into the bathroom. I heard the water running. She came out, her face washed clean of all make-up, her hair brushed soft and shining. "What happens now?"

"I don't know."

"Did Walter ... did he commit suicide because of what they told him about me?"

"No."

"Did he really commit suicide?"

"Yes. At least, I'm pretty sure."

"You've turned against me."

"Yes."

"You were under no great illusions about me. You have no reasons to be so bitter."

"No."

"I know, you'll go to confession on Sunday, and that will make everything all right again."

"Yes."

"What will they do to me?"

"Send you back to England."

"That's not so bad."

"No."

Things still weren't shaking out as they should. Walter had known his wife. None of these things should have surprised him. They didn't surprise me.

I brooded in silence, drinking. Maybe it was the whiskey that made me feel so bitter. Maybe.

She touched my arm and pushed my hair back out of my eyes. "Hungry?"

I realized I was famished. We went down to the Canadian Grill. I was a little under-dressed, but nobody said anything. I guess we were a bit early, so they figured nobody would see us. Then there was the fact that she looked like she belonged there.

I found the prices a bit steep, but it seemed normal to her. All the food seemed tasteless, but that was my fault, not the cook's. After paying, I was practically penniless again.

We went back to my room for a nightcap. Conversation had been desultory for the past hour.

We clinked glasses and toasted the future. She put her arm around my shoulder and whispered in my ear, "It's not so bad."

No, she was right. It wasn't so bad.

Again, she surprised me. I was treating her so badly, she should hate me. Instead, she unbuttoned my shirt and softly stroked my aching ribs.

I treated her roughly. At first, she protested. After awhile, she didn't.

CHAPTER 16

I was out on the streets a little before dawn. She was still asleep up in room 507. I walked slowly through the market area, hoping my ribs would stop aching soon. The farmers were setting up their stalls, some taking produce from horse-drawn carts, others emptying their trucks. I watched their efficiency and their good-natured friendliness. Right now, I'd rather be a farmer than a policeman.

I had a coffee and toast in a café that opened early for the farm trade. I smoked one of my cigarettes. The coughing made me hurt too much. I left the package on the counter when I left.

I sat in the Robinsons' room until the knock on the door came. I opened it.

I was not surprised to see Carson and the so-called ambassador there, come to take in the widow.

"Well, well. Come in, boys."

Carson was wary. "What you doing here? And where's Mrs. Robinson?"

I pulled the newspaper photo out of my pocket. "Nice to see you, Mister Ambassador. You do take a lousy picture, though."

Carson growled, "Peter Wilson, U.S. security."

"I'll accept the job description. The name, well, that's as may be."

Wilson tore the photo in half and threw it on the expensive carpet. He peered into the empty bedroom. "Duggan, you're a pain in the ass."

"That I am."

"I don't like you. I hope they get you for killing your wife."

Carson made soothing sounds. "Now, now, let's talk."

Wilson glared at me. "Yeah, let's talk. Understand, Duggan, the only reason I'm even considering talking to you is that you impressed us with that investigation into the Voscovitch killing. Finding out who she was and where she lived within twenty-four hours. That was good. But you're still a pain in the ass."

I sat on the chair, motioned them to the chesterfield. They both stayed where they were. "Yeah. I thought I was pretty good. Okay, let's talk. What should we talk about first? Voscovitch? I assume your guys killed her, Wilson."

"You assume wrong, Duggan. Maybe you're not as good as I thought you were."

"I told you that." Thanks a lot, Carson.

"How do you fit in, then?"

Wilson relaxed a bit, sat down. "We were running her. She wanted to defect, but we wanted more from her before we let her come over." He certainly had his own language. "I guess the Russians got wind of what was happening."

"So they were the ones killed her. The chauffeur?"

"Very good, Duggan, very good. I suppose so. He's the chief of intelligence operations."

"I had him in my hands one time. I let him go."

"Yeah, we heard. Too bad. The reason we were impressed with you is because we thought we had made it impossible to figure out who she was for a week or two."

"How did you do that?"

"We had her under surveillance all the time. But we lost her for a couple of hours the night she died. When we found her, she was already dead. So we moved her body, took all her I.D., dumped her in the park."

"So that's why she had no handbag or anything."

"Yeah. Your turn to give. How'd you get to her name and address so fast?"

"She called me the night she was killed. We had a meeting in the same park the next day."

"That bitch! She was doublecrossing us. Must have thought you'd give her a better deal."

"Sounds like doublecrosses all around."

"She gave you her name when you talked to her."

"No. Carson gave me that."

They exchanged murderous looks. Carson bleated, "I thought he already had the name. Same as you."

Wilson calmed him down. "Yeah, yeah, yeah. Who cares now?"

I cared. I cared a lot. "Let's skip a bit. Tell me, boys, how the hell does she fit in with Robinson? I'm going crazy with that one."

Carson took over. "Duggan, in a hundred years of investigation, you'd never figure that one out. It's way over your head."

"Try me. Don't forget, if she hadn't been killed, right now I'd be the guy who knew everything."

They exchanged looks. Which one would break first, I wondered.

It was Wilson. "We're still not sure, although I've got my own ideas. We would have done better if you hadn't came blundering in, Duggan."

"Me? What did I do?"

"You went to her apartment. We were outside, watching for whoever went in there. Figured it would tell us who had killed her. Then, out of the blue, who pops up but the Great Detective." He said that with a certain amount of sarcasm.

"Thanks for coming to my rescue."

"There was no chance of that. We don't even exist in this country. Much less run agents out of here."

I stood up and paced the floor. At least now I knew how Carson had found out so quickly about my beating. I needed more coffee, so I went into the kitchenette and rummaged about. I was finally starting to admit to myself that they were right, this was a hell of a lot more complicated than I had ever figured on.

"Coffee?" They both agreed to coffee, one black, one regular. I felt like the host.

"So, where is she, Duggan?" Carson's voice wafted into the kitchen.

"Not so fast, not so fast. She'll be here as soon as I tell her it's all right to come."

"Like her a lot, don't you, Duggan?"

"Yeah, I like her." I brought in the three coffees.

We all took up our cups, making the whole atmosphere more homey. I wandered over to the famous window. These guys were breaking my heart. So many lies, so much nonsense. And they still thought they were fooling me. I was depressed.

"So, tell me, Carson, how'd you convince him to write a note before he went over?"

"What're you talking about?" Carson was agitated.

"When I got here the day of his death, you were already here. How did you get here so fast? Don't tell me, I know. You walked down the steps from the seventh floor, came out the back door and walked around the hotel. Even if somebody had called you at work, you couldn't have been here that fast."

"You can't prove that, Duggan." He seemed very confident. He was right, I probably couldn't.

"Did he make you mad, Carson?"

Both Carson and Wilson seemed perplexed. Wilson spoke.

"Mad? How could he make him mad? Assuming he was even here that night."

"You challenged him to a little chess game, didn't you? You figured you'd while away the time convincing him to jump out the window by playing some chess. I bet you were terribly unhappy when he beat you in about a half-dozen moves. Offended your ego, didn't he?"

"He laughed at me. Said a six-year-old could do better." His eyes flashed at the memory.

I merely smiled. I had taken a shot in the dark about the chess game. Mind you, there weren't too many possibilities left. Carson turned his back to me. I moved closer.

"So, tell me. How did you convince him to write the note?"

"I don't know what you mean." He stared at me belligerently. Wilson sat still, sipping his coffee. He motioned with his head, either towards me or to the window itself, I wasn't sure. "Okay. It wasn't hard. He knew he had to go. Out the window, pills, a pistol against the temple, I didn't care. So long as it was a suicide. But you're wrong. I didn't help him, I swear!"

"You just convinced him."

"Yeah." Wilson was looking completely bored. I was just starting to get interested.

"I don't believe you. You either held a gun on him or helped him over the railing. Which one?"

Carson had a huge smile on his face. He came closer, his smile widening. "I guess it doesn't matter, anymore. It's all fixed now. Both."

"And she just watched it."

"The widow? No, she really was in bed. She's an old drunk. Like you." I considered taking a swing at him, but decided against it. "Maybe she heard voices, maybe she didn't. But she didn't want to know. She didn't care about him anyway. And I think he pretty well ignored her, too."

The voice of reason interceded from the chesterfield. "None of this really matters, does it? So what if Carson was here, Robinson did what was required, he jumped out the window. That's what happened, that's what the report on his death will say. There's no cover-up."

I wasn't so sure. I turned to Carson. "You know what convinced me something was wrong with the whole story?"

"No." He really didn't know.

"It was a good story. She may be a foolish bitch. She may have had communist connections. She may have had a communist lover. She may even have passed on messages innocently. But all that was sheer foolishness, it was stretching investigation beyond the bounds of decency. There was no reason to drag her into it. It took me until this morning to figure it out. She's no subversive."

"No." It was Wilson who agreed.

I heaved a sigh of relief. Now, I really could use a cigarette and didn't have any. "You got a smoke, Wilson?" He threw a pack of Camels over. I took one, threw the package back. "Okay, we got a Mountie watching while a diplomat jumps out a window. Why?"

"For real?" Wilson lit up.

"For real."

"Here it is." Carson sat beside Wilson. "Robinson was being blackmailed by the KGB."

I didn't believe him. "You're crazy!" Neither one of them looked crazy.

"No, it's true." Wilson blew smoke lazily into the air.

"What for?"

Carson stood again. "You never believe me when I tell you the truth, Duggan, but I'll try again. When Robinson was at Cambridge, he joined the Party. No pretend here. No common front, no study group, the real thing. He didn't keep it up, and he always denied it, but he joined up. It's a fact."

I tried a smoke ring. It didn't work. "So what? Lots of people did. They repented later, they were forgiven. It's not the end of the world."

Wilson blew a perfect smoke ring. "There's worse."

"What?"

"Sex. They had photos."

"Sex? You mean adultery."

Wilson snorted, leading him in a coughing fit. Carson smiled. "You might say."

I was confused. I thought I had everything all figured out, now I was more confused than ever. Sweet mother of Jesus, what were they on about? "What? What kind of sex?"

"You figure it out, Duggan."

Put that way, it took me about three seconds. "He was queer." In those days, they were queer, not homosexual and definitely not gay.

"Yeah." They spoke together.

"I see."

Carson took up the story. "Everywhere he went as a diplomat, he was passing on information. His wife had nothing to do with it. He was forced to pass over, or else the photos go to External. Maybe he did one good thing. He wasn't too ambitious, so he didn't get too high in the service. So he never had too much to betray. Maybe he did it on purpose."

"Was Voscovitch the person he was reporting to?"

"Probably. Maybe. Who knows? She fits in there somewhere. Doubt we'll ever know for sure."

Now I needed a drink. Things were making sense. Too much sense. "Okay, tell me this: how did the Americans find out?"

"I told them," Carson gloated.

"You?"

"Yeah, years ago. I didn't know it all, but I passed on what I knew."

"Nice guy."

"Doing my job."

Wilson interrupted. "That's right. Doing his job. At first, his facts were all wrong. But his intuition was right. Robinson was smelly, and Carson sniffed him out."

I was worried about only one thing. "His wife didn't know?"

"Not as far as we can tell. But she had her own little secrets."

"Poland."

Wilson was suddenly alert. "Poland? We don't know nothin' about Poland. What did she do there?"

I almost laughed. "Nothing that I know. Just that she was in a communist country, I figured..."

"Ya know, Carson, I bet he's right. I betcha there's somethin' in Poland we could dig up against her." He sounded almost gleeful. I wished I could keep my big mouth shut sometimes.

Carson interrupted. "Robinson's first three choices of postings were all places he could easily defect from."

"So? Let him defect. Solves the problem." I was glad to get away from the subject of Poland.

"You still don't understand. The prime minister has defended him. The minister of External Affairs has written to Washington on his behalf. A government could fall if he defected."

"And deserve it." I had no pity.

"Maybe. That's not your decision."

"And it's not your job to defend one particular political party over another. Let them go down." I surprised myself, me, a good Liberal saying something like that. But I meant it.

Carson meant what he was saying. "It's my job to hunt down traitors."

The sincerity in his voice made me have new thoughts. "I can almost see it now. You held a gun on him, didn't you? You said, 'It's a bullet or the window. And the window saves your reputation.'"

Wilson hadn't liked the note in Carson's voice, either. He put his hand on my elbow. "Now, now. We got the story. When we leave here, we want everyone happy."

I wasn't having any. "Didn't you?"

Carson sat and spoke very softly. "I wish I had. No, you're wrong. I was going to shoot him. He ran. He took the window himself. I couldn't stop him. I preferred a mysterious shooting, a burglary or something that would never be solved."

I prowled around, looking through the stock in the bar for something I could stomach. There was mostly champagne. Warm champagne didn't sound too good. There was some brandy. A bit of scotch. I took the scotch. I didn't offer it to them.

"I never liked you guys, you know. You run around with your goddamn red uniforms, you're so much better than the rest of us. I didn't see too many of you when I was overseas. Too busy tracking down subversives and beating up strikers. You guys make me sick." I was spent. I sat down with a large tumbler full of scotch. I hate scotch. Today it tasted good.

Carson loomed over me. "Okay, we make you sick. We do all the dirty jobs you don't like. Your heart bleeds for goddamn unionists and leftists. I got no problems with my conscience 'cause I hate both of 'em. And I'll lock 'em up any chance I get."

I've been depressed in my lifetime a good many times, but I can't remember a time when I felt more depressed than that one moment in that hotel room. I sighed deeply. Government people always think they know everything.

"I've still got a couple of questions. Either of you guys ever see the famous photos?"

"What photos?" Wilson was suddenly alert.

"The ones of Robinson and his friend in a compromising position."

They looked at each other. I knew then neither one had seen the photos.

"We don't need to see them. We know they exist."

"Well, lads, I'll tell you what I think. I think you've been set up. Set up twenty years ago by some real pros. I don't know why, and I don't know how. But right now I'll bet you my pension money you'll never find those pictures. If there's a Party membership card somewhere in Robinson's name, I bet you it's forged. I won't argue that there's no traitor in External, but I do think Robinson was set up to take the fall a long time ago.

"You guys helped an innocent man out of that window."

Both of them stood silent for a moment. Then Wilson let out a shrill laugh.

"You're crazy! Robinson was queer. And he was a commie."

I knew I'd never convince them. I also knew the only thin thread I had to tie together my line of reasoning was one comment from Gouzenko. It gave me small pleasure to know that these guys had been outwitted by the enemy years before they even knew the game was on. They were supposedly standing on guard for me, too. I moved closer to Carson, hissing through my teeth.

"So many stupidities! So many lies! You don't even know what you're up against." Carson glared into my face.

"It's not true. We got the guy dead to rights. Even if you were right—which I don't believe—you know what? I don't care. Our way is clean. It ties everything up. I'm sticking to our version."

Wilson came between us. "We're all law enforcement agents here." I laughed bitterly. He continued, "The way I figure it, we can all get together on this one."

Carson eyed him slyly. "How so?"

"Well, the way I see it, the commie bitch is dead, the traitor is dead, and the wife is on her way back to England. The only problem I see is how to write it up." Carson eyed him suspiciously, rightly so, I thought. "Duggan's got his own problems, what with his suspension and all, so maybe we should try to help him out."

I was instantly on the alert for betrayal. "How can you guys help me out?"

"I can't, but Carson here, can."

"I don't see how." I could tell by his face that Carson couldn't see how, either.

"Seems to me that if the Mounties admitted that you really solved both cases, you'd look good in Ottawa. And if you wrote up Robinson as a suicide and Voscovitch as probably being killed by her own people, both the Canadian and the American governments would be happy."

I snorted, "I'm glad somebody's going to be happy."

"There's another thing. Seems to me if the word came from on high, say from External or the senate, that the government would be terribly unhappy if your army record came out in public, you might be off of suspension p.d.q."

"P.d.q. I like that." I didn't think it would need their help, but it couldn't hurt, either.

"So, is it a deal?"

"What do you think, Carson?"

"Can't hurt me. Shake?"

"I don't think I want to shake on this one. I don't consider it a deal. It's just street-cleaning, that's all."

Wilson wasn't miffed, not a bit. He stared Carson down. "So long as we're all agreed."

Carson still wasn't happy. "The way I figure, if you're gonna go along with this, you got no right to come onto me so self-righteous, the way you do."

"You still don't get it, do you, Carson?"

"No, I don't."

Wilson was at the door. "Leave it, Carson. We got what we wanted. Leave the rest. Except for one thing. Where is she, Duggan?"

"This is the guy who wasn't going to pull no doublecross." Carson sounded bitter.

"She'll be here in five minutes." I closed the door softly behind me.

She answered my knock all bleary-eyed, rubbing the sleep from her eyes. "You look all bright-eyed and bushy-tailed," she yawned.

"Bright-eyed, maybe." She put her arms around me and kissed my cheek. "I don't feel so bushy-tailed."

"You need a shave."

"That I do."

She sat dolefully on the bed, her shoulders sagging.

"What's happening now?"

"They're waiting upstairs."

"They?"

"Carson and an American agent I don't think you've met."

"Will they brow-beat me?"

"I doubt it. If they ask, don't mention Viktor. They've never heard of Viktor."

"I'm glad."

I guess I was glad too. At least there was something to be glad about. Viktor would be just one more story that would never be told.

Martha gathered her handbag and stood looking around the room. "It's not much." She could have been referring to anything. "I guess they'll ask me a lot of questions."

"I think they'll be more anxious to get you out of the country."

"I suppose so." She draped her handbag over her shoulder. "Poor Walter, I wasn't very good for him."

"Nor he for you."

"We were in love, almost twenty years ago. It's funny how it can slip away. You don't think so at the time."

"No."

"So, has your talk with Sergeant Carson and this American convinced you that Walter committed suicide?"

"I'm afraid not."

"Will you ever give up trying to find the truth?"

I didn't even try to fool her. "Yep. I've already given up. Oh, I know pretty much of the truth. Carson was there that night. He made it pretty clear that Walter had to die. The only choice he had was the method of his death."

"Can he get away with that?"

"I guess so. There'll never be any evidence to the contrary. You and I both know it's not the truth. But on paper it will have to say suicide while of unsound mind."

"But why? I still don't see why."

"The claim is that he was being blackmailed by the KGB."

"Over what?"

"Some homosexual affair he had long ago." She looked so sad. Not surprised, just sad.

"Poor Walter. If it's true that he had a male lover one time, I'm sure he found the whole incident tawdry and shameful. He probably never even did it again."

"Once was enough, if it was with the wrong person."

"Someone should warn..." she trailed off abruptly.

"Who?"

"Nobody in particular." She turned away from me. "I was just thinking of all the other diplomats."

I took her by the shoulder and spun her around to face me. I tried to stare her down for a long moment. "You're thinking of one particular person. I know that. If I wasn't so tired and beat-up, I'd get the name out of you. But I'm too old and worn-out today."

"Thank you for that. I guess I knew Walter as well as any wife knows her husband. I'm not sure I believe these people."

"Nor am I, Martha, nor am I. It might be true, they claim they have evidence. But then again, I'd believe whatever I wanted to believe."

She shuddered, standing close beside me. I felt like touching her, but I didn't. She turned away abruptly. I moved towards the door. She put her hand on the doorknob and turned it slowly.

"Well, let's go up."

"Yeah. Let's go."

"Will we ever meet again?"

"No."

"Does that make you sad?"

"Yeah." Lots of things make me sad.

"Will you think of me often?"

"Yeah."

"Promise?"

"I promise. Martha." I took her hand in the elevator.

I brought her to the door of her room. She hugged me, tears in her eyes. "How should I play it, Pen?"

"You're the innocent wife. That's the only way to play it."

"That sounds good. Thank you."

"Don't thank me. It's not necessarily a thankful role."

"It'll do. The innocent wife. I like that. I haven't thought of myself in that way for a long time."

"Glad you like it."

She knocked on the door. Carson and Wilson let her in, then slammed the door in my face. "Get lost, Duggan."

I got lost.

CHAPTER 17

All that was more than thirty years ago. Now, I live in a high-rise apartment on Wurtemburg Street, looking down onto what was once Lowertown. In a way, I got my wish. They tore down the whole neighbourhood and replaced it with identical little apartment blocks. I think they call them condominiums. I was right about one thing. The people don't seem to be any happier.

Now that I think back on it, maybe it wasn't the summer of 1954 that was so goddamned hot. Maybe the heat wave was the year before that, or a few years after. I find my memory is good for some things, but not so good for others. Lots of memories seem to collide against each other.

Most everybody in this story is dead now, except for me. Bruno had a heart attack just two months ago. He died not knowing I had seen him coming out of my apartment building that night in 1946. He tried the best he could to make up for his betrayal of me without ever admitting to it. Back then, he hadn't known me well enough to make it a serious betrayal of friendship. It's funny that I could become his pal later, knowing what I knew. It's funny and sad at the same time.

I don't know about Martha. I lied, of course. I didn't think of her often. In the first couple of months I dreamt about her. It was a welcome change from dreaming about Lucille.

Carson became assistant commissioner of the RCMP many years later. Robinson's friend John Watkins, the ambassador to Moscow, eventually admitted he had been blackmailed for years by the KGB over a homosexual affair he had with a young Muscovite.

Ed Lukowicz and his wife were killed in a head-on collision with a drunk driver in 1966.

Igor Gouzenko died in his sleep a few years ago. When I met him, I didn't much care for him, but he might have been right about the blackmail story, or the story that was supposed to look like blackmail. It makes me smile the odd time speculating that maybe Gouzenko was right, maybe the KGB only made it look like Robinson was being blackmailed, and he was innocent all the while. Innocent, but unable to make anyone believe him. So he had to take the high dive from the seventh storey.

I guess it doesn't really matter anymore. Robinson's dead and so is Gouzenko.

I have a great-nephew and his wife who come to visit me every couple of weeks. They used to take me for rides in their car, but after awhile I found it depressing. I didn't recognize the city anymore.

I find myself explaining too much how it was in those days. How attitudes were different then.

I find myself regretting so many things I did in those days.

I find myself walking in the park and getting tired before I've even made one tour of the pathway.

I find myself remembering.

They dropped the charges against me, of course. Seems there was a lot of pressure. I put in the rest of my days until retirement. I had a good long run of a perfect record on murder investigations until the 1960s. After that, it seemed like every second murder in the city went unsolved. There were a lot more of them, too. After awhile, cops became as useful at making people behave in a civilized manner as trombone players were. Maybe I should have tried to get a job with Artie Shaw.

I wrote up the two deaths like we had agreed. I slipped in a few more maybes than they would have liked, but that's all. It no longer mattered to me whether Robinson was a commie or a queer or not. So long as I knew that Carson was responsible for his death, I felt all right about making up a story about suicide. I didn't say that it was Carson who had played chess with

Robinson that night. In my report I speculated that it was somebody so high up in the government that we were better off not knowing. Nobody liked that line, but they let it pass.

I worked with the Mounties a time or two in later years, but I never learned to like them any better. When the politicians and the civil servants and the Mounties get together in the interests of national security, there's not much you and I can do about it. Robinson died so a government wouldn't fall. That's enough for me.

Now I sit here waiting to die, and I think of poor Lucille all the time. Maybe I should have confessed to her murder and let them hang me.

No, Duggan, that's foolish. That wouldn't have punished you enough. The only suitable punishment is to go to an old man's death with your soul condemned to damnation forever.

To hell with it, then. I wonder what's on television now.